1.75

The Bon Air Boys

The Bon Air Boys Adventures

WHISPERS

IN

THE WIND

BY

GREG W. GOLDEN

This book is not intended to endorse or promote any of the activities by the characters contained therein. Any similarity between locations or these characters to actual places or those persons living or dead is coincidental.

The Author

Acknowledgements

My motivation in writing The Bon Air Boys series of books came from the many hours spent with our first grandchild, a wonderful little boy named Grant. The world he is growing up in and the one of my childhood are vastly different. The influences that will pull on him are more complex than those I faced, but his options and mine are much the same. Grant can either be shaped by his world, or he can be a world-shaper!

For the reader, I hope to encourage values that are rooted in kindness, truth, loyalty, forgiveness, and a spirit of adventure in every day!

As an ordained minister, I see each sunrise as a new set of opportunities to live in God's wonderful light and love! If my outlook can be contagious, I have accomplished my mission.

My thanks in this endeavor go to my dear wife and tireless editor, Debbie; to our sons Andrew and Jonathan and their wives Christina and Emily. They all encouraged me and assisted in refining this book into what you are seeing. Our grandchildren Grant, Iris, and Ellie inspire me in their own ways daily.

Thank you, Melinda, for your valuable input—always!

Even though we've never met, thank you to Pastor Mark Batterson of National Community Church in Washington, D.C. Your obedience to write *In A Pit With A Lion On A Snowy Day* challenged me toward my own obedience to pen the Bon Air Boys books.

About The Author

Greg Golden grew up in middle America, the youngest of three children and the only son of a pastor. Greg's love for literature was first demonstrated when at the age of ten he ran out of the forty-three Hardy Boys books available to read and he wrote one for himself.

After college, his career path took him to Mobile, Alabama, where he met and married Debbie. There they raised two sons, and those sons and wives have given them numerous grandchildren—the newest loves and diversions in their lives.

Greg is an ordained minister, and he frequently mentors those seeking encouragement and guidance which come across his path.

Contents

Chase stopped and shined his flashlight in front of him, swinging the beam around in search of the next mark of red paint. "Guys, I think we're off the trail. I must have missed one of the paint marks. I don't know how far off we are, but we better back up and try to find the trail again."

No sooner had those words left his mouth than each boy felt an electrical charge in the air. The hair on their arms seemed to stand on end, and an explosion overhead sent a shock of lightning down a tree only a half dozen yards from where they stood. Bark, cinders, and sparks flew from the trunk—some landing just a few feet from the boys. The strength of nature's fireworks made their ears ring and nearly pushed the boys to the ground.

From "Whispers In The Wind"

Whispers In The Wind

A CALL FOR HELP

Chapter 1

Chase Spencer slowly turned the dial on his shortwave radio receiver. The static in the earphones told him that somewhere in the distance, a nighttime thunderstorm was underway. He paused and listened briefly at each instance of a voice or music. The time was just after 11 o'clock. He had planned to be in bed by 10, but for some reason, he wasn't tired.

He switched the selector on his radio to a different frequency band. Through the magic of the copper wire antenna strung between trees in his backyard, distant people speaking in other languages reached into his room. He was captivated by those faraway places. Chase imagined their distant cultures as he listened to Radio Netherlands and the BBC from London. He wondered who else in another part of the world was doing the same thing at the same moment.

A 40-watt bulb in his gooseneck desk lamp illuminated a corner of the bedroom. The orange glow of the radio dial reflected in his eyes. A small, electric fan with its chromed blade guard hummed and slowly turned back and forth. It stirred the night air that drifted through his open window.

Charles Spencer lightly tapped on his son's bedroom door. With headphones covering his ears, Chase didn't hear the knock. The door opened. "Don't forget that you have a dentist appointment in the morning."

Chase removed the headphones. "All right, Dad. I'm about to shut this off for the night. Thanks for reminding me."

"I'll need to leave early to open the store since Mr. Williamson is on vacation this week. I won't be here to wake you."

"That's fine, Dad. Goodnight."

The door closed. Chase turned back to his shortwave radio and switched to a new band of frequencies. A few moments later, as he slowly rotated the tuner dial, he heard an anxious voice in the middle of an urgent call.

"....at the six-mile marker. We're losing pressure. I'm trying to make it as far as Lewisville, and I need to sidetrack there. Anybody reply, please! We have an emergency! Can anyone hear me? Over."

All thoughts of bedtime were suddenly gone, and Chase was instantly wide awake! Someone somewhere was in danger, and nobody was answering his anxious call.

"Dad! *Dad!*"

There was no response.

After a moment, Chase unplugged his headphones, and the radio speaker came to life. *"This is westbound Fletcher Railway 1611. We've blown a boiler, and we're going to need to sidetrack. Just passed the five-mile marker approaching Lewisville. I need a switchman ahead to help! Can anyone hear me? Over."*

The caller's voice was even more frantic this time. A train

without power was coasting toward Lewisville, and the urgency was clear to Chase. Unless someone from the railroad responded and pushed the correct switch at the Lewisville yard, the crippled train and its passengers would block the only track that ran through town. The midnight mail train was expected soon. In the dark of night and with this failure of communications, a collision on the track was almost certain!

His father flung open the door. *"What is it, son? What do you need?"*

"Dad, I just heard an emergency call on my radio! It's a train coming into town without any engine power. Something has happened to their boiler. They're trying to get somebody in the switchyard to answer, but no one has."

Before Chase's dad could react, the anxious voice blasted through the speaker. *"This is an emergency! We need help! If anyone can hear me, contact the Lewisville Rail Yard! They must switch us to a sidetrack. We're slowing down, but something has to happen within a few minutes. We're four miles out. Over!"*

The situation was clear to both of them. Mr. Spencer stepped back into the second-floor hall and picked up the receiver on the upstairs telephone. He dialed zero for the Operator, then returned through the open door of Chase's bedroom.

"Operator, this is an emergency! Connect me with the Fletcher Railroad—the Switchman's Station—at the Lewisville Rail Yard. Hurry, please!"

Both Chase and his father looked at one another in the

silence of what was only fifteen seconds but felt like several minutes. Mr. Spencer's expression changed as a voice came through the telephone handset.

"Yes, this is Charles Spencer. You have an inbound train that has declared an emergency. It has lost its power and is coasting into Lewisville. We just heard their distress call on shortwave radio, and they need you to switch them off the mainline onto your sidetrack."

Chase couldn't understand any of the person's response, but he heard the excited tone coming from the phone pressed against his father's ear.

"That's all we know," his dad continued. "The engineer sounded very concerned. Can you help him? Can you do what he's asking?"

"It's train 1611, Dad," Chase whispered.

"It is number 1611," Mr. Spencer repeated into the telephone. "He should be there to you in just a few minutes."

There was a pause, and no one spoke for a half-minute.

Chase's dad pulled the mouthpiece away from his lips and whispered to Chase. "It's apparently against regulations to put an unscheduled train onto a sidetrack, but because the engineer said it's an emergency..." He abruptly stopped speaking to Chase.

"Okay, great! Thank you. Yes. You are very welcome. All right. Goodnight."

He stepped back into the hallway and placed the phone

handset on its base.

"Chase, I don't know how you happened to hear that message, but I think you may have saved some people a lot of problems and maybe more than that. The mail train is due to pass through town—probably in the next half-hour. I hate to think what might have happened if they weren't able to clear a broken-down train sitting there on the main track."

"I was just tuning around on my radio, and I heard that man trying to get someone to answer him. I'm glad that you knew what to do."

"Let's both try to get some sleep, son. I'll leave some cinnamon toast and some fresh fruit out for you and your brother when I leave. Is your alarm set?"

"Yes, sir. Thanks, Dad. I'm glad Aunt Carol is getting better, and Mom and Sally are coming home. You're an okay cook, but Mom is the best!"

"Amen to that! Be sure to pray for your aunt. She's had a tough time in these last months. Goodnight, son—again!"

Chase switched off the shortwave receiver, double-checked his alarm clock, turned off the desk lamp, and crawled into the bottom bunk bed.

The tabletop fan's breeze moved gently across him, back and forth. Although his body was tired, his mind was wide awake from the anxious moments he had just experienced. He prayed silently for his aunt. He thought about the events of the day and his conversation earlier with Frank and Griff over their walkie-talkies.

His younger brother Matthew coughed once and then rolled over in the top bunk. He had slept through all of the excitement.

While locusts buzzed their muffled chatter in the maple trees, sleep slowly came. Chase's last memory of the first Tuesday in August was the distant whistle of the midnight mail train as it passed safely through Lewisville.

....

"Who's ready for some Frisbee?" asked a familiar voice in a volume twice as loud as a usual conversation. Chase awakened with a jump at the sound and then cracked one eye open to see a fuzzy version of Griff Jenkins standing in his open bedroom door.

"Uh, I—I have a dentist appointment at 9 o'clock. I can probably meet up with you after that." Chase raised on his elbows and reached behind him, folding his pillow to prop up his head.

"I think you overslept a little bit, buddy. It's 10:30."

Panic, like a jolt of electricity, shot through Chase. In a single motion, he swung his legs out from the bed covers and stood. Out of everyone he knew, his own family included, he alone was *never* late. He made it his mission *always* to arrive a minute or two early whenever and wherever he was expected. In the 6th grade Chase received the *On Time* award from his elementary school principal. He had never been tardy, and he was on track to have perfect attendance through all of his years in school.

"I was just teasing," Griff admitted. "It's just 8:15. You can relax. You're fine." He smiled and then braced himself for the expected shoulder punch from one of his two best friends, the other one being Frank Whidden.

"You nearly gave me a heart attack, but I'll forgive you anyway," Chase said while forcing a half-sincere smile. He turned around and saw that Matthew wasn't in the top bunk.

"Your brother was in the kitchen eating breakfast when I came in," Griff explained. "I think he might have left a *little* food for you. Everything looked pretty tasty, and Matthew acted mighty hungry."

"Give me a few minutes to get dressed, and I'll be right down. And tell Matt that half of whatever food Dad fixed is supposed to be for me!"

"All right, but I'd hurry if I were you. I don't think Matt realizes that." Griff grinned and pulled the bedroom door closed behind him.

....

The two buddies mounted their bicycles and pedaled down Chase's driveway. "Matt must have heard the alarm clock and turned it off for me, so I'm *really* glad that you came by, Griff. I guess he didn't realize that I planned to get up early and go into town."

As they rode together, Chase told Griff about the distress call. "It was pretty crazy last night," Chase continued while they coasted toward the town square of Lewisville, their hometown of 11,000. "It felt almost like I was in a movie when I heard that emergency call on my shortwave radio.

I kept thinking that somebody else was going to jump in and offer to help, but nobody did."

"Wow! This is the first I've heard about it. It seems like maybe you saved the day. I'm proud of you, Chase! It would have been pretty bad if that train couldn't get onto the sidetrack before another one came through town."

"Are you sure you don't mind waiting for me at the dentist office? It's just a check-up, so it shouldn't take very long," Chase asked.

"It's all good. I swung by Frank's house on the way to yours, but he'd gone into town a little while earlier. Maybe we'll run into him, and we can talk him into some Frisbee time, too."

Griff and Chase were two blocks from City Hall as the bell tower there gonged the quarter-hour of 8:45. "I told you you'd be fine," Griff said.

Turning the corner in front of them on the opposite side of the street and pedaling toward the two friends was Frank, the third Bon Air boy. Behind him on both sidewalks and in the town square was a large group of people—many more than typical on a Wednesday morning.

"Hey Frank," Griff shouted to their approaching friend. All three boys came to a stop. "What's going on in the square? Where did all those people come from?"

"You haven't heard?" he asked.

"Heard what? I've only been up for half an hour," Chase explained.

Before Frank could respond, an elephant emerged from a crossing street and lumbered across their path. Griff and Chase stood wide-eyed at that sight.

"A train broke down last night and had to stop here," Frank reported. "It's the Bingham Circus train, and it looks like they're going to be stuck in town for a while."

....

STRANGER IN THE SHADOWS

Chapter 2

"This is *unbelievable*," Chase said, staring in amazement at the nine-foot-tall, six-ton animal.

"There are a whole lot more where this one came from," Frank explained. "If you can sort of picture in your mind Noah's Ark, that's what it looks like between here and the railroad yard. They're moving them as fast as they can to the County Fairgrounds. I saw your dad near here a while ago, Griff. Some of his deputies have blocked off the side roads. They're trying to keep traffic from scaring the horses and the animals that aren't in cages. It's pretty crazy stuff right now."

Griff looked at Chase and punched him in the shoulder. "You had a big part in this, buddy! It wasn't just *people* that you helped. This circus is *famous*!"

"How are you connected with all of this, Chase?" Frank asked.

Chase spoke in Frank's direction while watching the parade of cages, riders on horseback, and small and tall people herding animals of every color, type, and description. "Last night on my radio receiver I heard an emergency message by the engineer or someone from that train. My dad made a phone call, and he reached the switchman at the rail yard. They were able to get the train moved away from the mainline. I had no idea it was *this* kind of a train."

"Our Chase is a *hero!*" Griff proclaimed as he patted him on the back.

"You are crazy, and *I'm* about to be late," Chase replied. He turned to Frank and asked, "You want to join us in the park for some Frisbee in about thirty minutes? I have a quick dentist appointment, and then I'm free after that."

"Sure! Count me in!"

"We'll wait for you over there," Griff said to Chase, pointing to a park bench on the edge of the town square.

....

The half-hour chime from the clock above City Hall sounded, but Chase wasn't anywhere in sight. Another several dozen workers and cast members of the Bingham Circus made up the end of the procession as they headed on foot to the fairgrounds southwest of Lewisville. Frank and Griff watched the final circus carts and animals pass by. Activity around the square was finally quiet, and town life felt normal again.

"*I'm coming!*" Chase yelled and waved from a half-block away. The other two boys stood and straddled their bikes. Suddenly, Chase stopped in the middle of the road and got off his bike. He lowered the kickstand and leaned over to examine something he noticed on the street. He reached down, picked up a small item, studied it, and then slipped it into his jeans pocket. Chase then walked his bike the last two hundred feet to meet Frank and Griff.

"What did you find?" Frank asked.

"I don't know. I don't exactly recognize it. It *looks* like a key, but it's an odd shape." He propped his bike against his leg and pulled the brass item from his pocket. "There's a hole in it, I guess for a key ring, but nothing else to show what it belongs to or whose it is."

Each boy held the metal item and examined it. It seemed familiar to them, but no one was certain how or where it was used.

"My dad's store is just around the corner on the way to the Frisbee field. We can stop there and see if he recognizes it," Chase suggested.

Spencer Hardware was a popular business in downtown Lewisville. When a person stepped inside, he got an immediate feeling that somewhere on a shelf or in a corner, he could find the items he needed to construct or fix whatever needed to be built or repaired. Chase's grandfather had opened the store forty-five years earlier. His dad operated the hardware by himself after the elder Spencer retired. From snow shovels to fertilizer and from furnace filters to snapdragon seeds—it was all there, neatly organized and well-presented.

The bell attached to the coiled spring above the door dinged loudly as the three boys entered.

Charles Spencer stood up from kneeling in front of a display of bicycle tire patches. "Hey there, fellows! Chase, how was your dentist check-up?"

"I got a good report! No cavities again!"

"Good for you! So, what brings you three down here?"

"I found this, Dad. It was in the middle of the street. I *think* I've seen something like it before, but I don't remember where." He handed his dad the brass item.

"It's a key—*that much* I can say for sure. But it's not for an ordinary lock. It would fit a storage locker like the ones you'd find at a bus station or a train station," Mr. Spencer said confidently. "In the street? That's where you found it?"

"Right in the middle," Chase responded.

"I'd expect there to be a number stamped onto a tag and for there to be a metal ring connecting the key to the tag," Mr. Spencer noted. "That's an important part because there could be dozens, maybe a hundred lockers at our bus and train stations. And, what's more, I can't be sure it's for the type of lock found at either of those places here in town."

Griff spoke up. "I have an idea. Let's go back and look around the place where the key was. Maybe the tag got separated from the key there. The animals, the rolling cages, the people—all of those went past that same spot. Someone from the train could have dropped it, and maybe we can get it back to the owner."

"Yeah," Frank continued, "and we can go by the Sheriff's office, Griff, and see if your dad knows about anyone who reported it missing."

"Those are both excellent ideas, fellows," Mr. Spencer acknowledged. "I'm sure that it's a locker key. Beyond that, you're on your own, I'm afraid."

"Thanks, Dad," Chase said as the three of them returned to the entrance and walked outdoors into the sunshine.

The automobile traffic was light on the street, and it took the friends only a few minutes to search the area for the key tag. They walked a half-block on the street in both directions looking along the curbs. In several places where they searched there were inlets for stormwater to drain. They couldn't rule out the possibility that a key tag might have been kicked or dropped into one of those openings.

Finding nothing, they rode their bicycles two blocks farther to the Jeffers County Sheriff's Office, parked them near the front door, and walked in.

From behind the closed door to Sheriff Lee Jenkins' office, a loud voice filled the room.

"Why can't you arrest him?" barked the angry man. The back of the person speaking was all that was visible to them through the glass portion of the office door.

Lee Jenkins, by contrast, was not speaking loud enough for them to hear. The boys could see that the Sheriff was calm, trying to satisfy the upset stranger. Suddenly the short, dark-haired man spun around. He grabbed the knob, flung the door open, and weaved his way through several desks in the large room. *"This won't be the last time you see me!"* he ranted as he shoved past the three boys and left the building.

The half-dozen workers, clerks, and deputies across the room all looked up from their desks at the same time. Their expressions were almost identical. They showed disbelief over the man's rage, and admiration that the

Sheriff had been so professional and calm.

"Hello, boys," a pleasant Lee Jenkins said. "Come on into my office. What can Jeffers County do for you today?"

Everyone in the room breathed a collective sigh. Their quiet laughter signaled that the crisis of the moment was over.

"Wow! Good for you, Dad!" said Griff as the three walked past the outer desks and stepped inside the Sheriff's private office.

"Chase found this key," Griff began. "It was in the middle of the street right where the circus people walked when they went to the Fairgrounds. We don't know exactly where it came from, but we thought someone might be looking for it."

Frank continued. "Mr. Spencer said he's sure that it's from a storage locker, like the ones at the bus or train station. We wanted to leave it with you in case anyone came to claim it."

"All right, guys, I'll log it into our system and leave it with the receptionist. Someone will probably stop by and ask about it. Thank you for being alert, Chase, and noticing it."

The boys left the Sheriff's building, but not before Lee Jenkins mussed his son Griff's thick mop of hair, as he often did.

Outside again, as the boys mounted their bicycles, a small man with a bushy mustache and dark sunglasses backed into the shadows alongside the Municipal Water Service building across the street from the Sheriff's office. Chase saw the man, but looked away quickly, pretending not to notice him at all. He had an odd feeling about the encounter, but he put it aside. As they headed for the Frisbee field at Snyder Park, Chase suddenly remembered seeing that same man watching them from among the trees in the Town Square while the boys searched the street for the key tag. He was sure of it.

....

After throwing the Frisbee back and forth—and climbing trees more than once to shake the toy platter out of low limbs—they sat down and rested in the shade.

"It still seems like a crazy dream—that call on the radio from the train," Chase reflected. "I don't believe anything happens by chance, and I guess it will all make sense one day."

"I don't know about you two, but the heat and this game have wiped me out. Let's head over there and get a drink, and then go to my house for a little while," Griff suggested. He pointed to a covered pavilion with restrooms and water fountains.

As they rode their bicycles in the direction of Griff's house in Bon Air Village, their route took them past the Faith Family Church. To their surprise, the parking lot was buzzing with activity as people carried food of all types, jugs of tea, packages of paper plates, and stacks of napkins from their cars into the fellowship hall.

"Let's check it out," Frank suggested. "I don't remember

hearing about any meal at church scheduled for today or tonight. Do you?"

None of them could guess the reason for the many cars and dozens of people continuing to file into the building. They parked their bikes and noticed Matt, Chase's brother, standing outside the door. "We're putting all of this food into coolers and taking lunch to the fairgrounds for the Bingham Circus folks," Matt said. "They're going to be here for a few days while their train is being repaired."

Their church regularly found ways to express kindness to the people of Lewisville. The Bible's command to "Love your neighbor as yourself" was their motivation to serve all the members of their community. Faith Family Church had grown and prospered since Reverend Bill Metcalfe had begun leading the congregation with the attitude of being generous toward others with their time and talents.

"Griff, can you three help us inside for a few minutes? We're starting to load the church vans, and we need some strong boys over here." The speaker was Griff's mother, Barbara Jenkins.

"You got it, Mom!" Griff replied as he motioned his friends toward the entrance.

The hastily-assembled kitchen crew in the fellowship hall worked in harmony, and they had filled many insulated coolers and large ice chests. Each had a strip of white tape with handwritten labels stating *Meat, Vegetables*, or *Dessert*. A white-haired lady stacked loaves of bread in cardboard boxes. The boys joined Reverend Metcalfe and several dads along with some retired men carrying the food for loading. The volunteers stowed jugs of tea and water into two church vans wherever an available space could be found. Two pickup trucks were filled with folding tables, and an empty hay wagon had been fitted with wooden sides. Chairs were stacked on the hay wagon from one end to the other.

"Would you boys ride with us and help set up to distribute the food?" Gene Walters, the Music Pastor asked Frank and the others.

"Of course!"

"I'll drive you back. It shouldn't take more than an hour. We'll leave the tables and chairs with them while the folks are staying at the fairgrounds."

....

In their wildest imaginations Griff, Frank, and Chase couldn't have prepared themselves for what they saw as their food caravan reached the County Fairgrounds. In the space of fewer than twelve hours, circus workers had erected an enormous red and white big-top tent next to the rodeo area. People moved like ants in and out of the tent carrying their belongings and pushing rolling cages that contained lions, tigers, and bears. Elephants were lined up and secured inside the rodeo fencing. It all looked like organized chaos to the townspeople of Lewisville, but it was the normal day-to-day life of the Bingham Circus.

The vans, pickups, and hay wagon pulled alongside the edge of the big-top, and the team from the church began to unload the tables, chairs, and food.

"This is amazing, Mom," Griff remarked, his face beaming

with excitement.

"I know," she replied. "It feels so good when you can serve someone who has no way to repay you."

As the last containers of food were being unloaded, Chase grabbed both handles of a large picnic cooler and struggled to hold onto it. He quickly set it back on the floor of the van so he could get a better grip. As he did, he had the odd feeling that someone had stepped behind him.

"I'll halp you vis dis." The deep voice and thick accent startled him, but Chase was sure that the look on his face showed *much more* than surprise as he turned. Face-to-face with him was the mustached man from the shadows.

....

ANOTHER CLUE SURFACES

Chapter 3

"Thank you, sir," Chase replied. He glanced around looking for his friends, hoping to find Frank or Griff nearby. Although Chase felt uneasy at first, the stranger didn't seem threatening, and he actually had a gentle manner. Each of them held a handle of the cooler, and they easily moved the container to a nearby table.

"I didun't mean to frighten you! You reminds me of mein own zon, but he'z older than you. He left us and I'm looking around here for him."

"That's okay. I'm sorry about that, sir. Has he been away for long?" Chase inquired.

"He vas angry ven he left home, und I don't know vere he vent. We love him, and I haft been trying to find him."

Frank stepped next to Chase and tapped on his arm. "Our ride is ready to take us back to the church. Griff and I are finished. Can you come now?"

"Uh, sure. Just a second." He turned toward the stranger. "Did you come on the train, too—with the circus?"

"I followed ze train pecauze I tought mein son might be vorking vith zem. I shtopped here in mein car vhen zee train came last night."

"Well, I hope that you find him, sir. I need to go now.

Maybe we'll see you later."

As they turned toward the church van, the stranger spoke anxiously again. "His name is Eric Schneider if vu effer zee him."

"Okay. I'll keep my eyes open for Eric, Mr. Schneider. We need to go now."

Chase boarded the church van and watched through the window as the small, moustached man walked to the outer edge of the crowd. He silently scanned the circus people who were under the big-top waiting for the pot-luck meal. As the van bumped and rattled toward the exit of the fairground property, Mr. Schneider turned around empty-handed and walked to his car.

"Who were you talking with?" Frank asked as the three friends and other church volunteers turned onto the main highway.

"It was sad," Chase began. "Two times today I saw that man watching us. The first time was when we were looking for the key tag, and then I saw him again when we were leaving the Sheriff's office. He's trying to find his boy. He told me that I reminded him of his son."

....

Most evenings at 8 o'clock, the three Bon Air boys talked with each other using the walkie-talkies they kept in their bedrooms. Their homes were within a couple of blocks of the others in the Bon Air Village neighborhood on the east side of Lewisville.

"Breaker, breaker! Are you guys on your radios?" Griff asked.

"I'm here," Frank reported.

Within a few seconds Chase joined the conversation. "We ate a late supper, and I just finished. What's up, guys?"

Griff replied. "Chase, I told my dad about that man—Mr. Schneider. He said he would check the registry of missing persons and see if an Eric with that last name shows up. They keep those files in his office on microfilm, and he'll take a look tomorrow."

"That sounds great," Chase replied. "Mr. Schneider seemed a little scary to me at first, but he was as nice as he could be once we began talking."

"I wish we could help him," Frank added. "Maybe if your dad locates a photo, Griff, we can be on the lookout for Eric, even after the train leaves."

Chase asked a question of his buddies. "Do you guys have plans for tomorrow afternoon? There's a matinee movie showing at 2:00 and again at 6:00 at the Rialto. Would either of you like to go see it with me? It's that one about a ship in World War II that runs aground near Italy."

"I'm due at Mr. Rigsby's at noon, so I better not try for the 2:00 one. I probably wouldn't be ready in time. Is the 6:00 showing okay with you two?" Frank asked.

"Sounds fine with me," Griff said. "Would you all want to come back to my house when the movie's over? We won't have had supper, so I can ask my folks to order some pizzas for us. We can hang out here afterward and play pool or just goof off."

"I'll check with my parents, too," Frank replied. "It should be fun. I'm sure they won't mind."

Griff felt that his mom and dad would be agreeable, and they ended the conversation saying that they would consider it confirmed unless the others learned something different by mid-morning.

"Hey, before we all sign-off, let's pray for Mr. Schneider and his son," Chase suggested. "It would be so cool if they could find each other here in town. I'll pray."

"God, we believe that you always know what's going on, and you care for all of us. If there was something that went bad with their relationship, we ask you to fix it and allow Mr. Schneider and his son to patch things up and get back together again. If you can use us to help, we are willing to do whatever we can. Amen."

"'Night, everybody. I'll see you guys at the Rialto at 5:45 tomorrow," Frank said.

Griff added, "Ditto that!"

....

Leonard Rigsby lived in a house that was unlike any other home in Bon Air Village. Frank's parents had been friends with the widower in his mid-80s for many years. Even though they weren't related, he was family in every sense of the word—much like an adopted third grandfather. Frank and his college-aged sister Kate often looked for ways to help him. Frank did yard work or small tasks, and Kate drove Mr. Rigsby to the market or to doctor appointments.

On this day, all Frank knew about going by and helping him was from a note that his mom taped to his bedroom door. It simply said to *"Go see Mr. Rigsby at noon."*

The summer day began hotter than usual, so Frank dressed for the morning in a t-shirt, cargo shorts, and sneakers. He felt it wasn't already time to mow the spacious yard. He had done that less than a week ago—however, he wanted to be dressed comfortably in case the job for the day was an outdoor one.

Frank arrived on his bike and laid it down in the grass of the front yard. As he reached the steps of the three-story home with its four white columns, he noticed Mr. Rigsby was seated on the porch swing. Next to him was a small, wooden box—one of a size that could barely hold an apple.

"Hello, Frank! I'm glad that you could come today."

"It's always good to see you, Mr. Rigsby. What is the project of the day that I can help you with?"

"Project? Oh, that's not why I called and asked your mother if you would stop by. I don't have any projects for you today. Instead, I have something that I want to give you—I want it to be yours. It's something that I value very much, and I hope that you will enjoy it now." He extended his arms and handed the small, hinged box to Frank. "Go ahead. Open it, son." Leonard Rigsby smiled and folded his hands on his lap.

Frank turned the box around in his hands and admired its beautiful construction with its brass hinges and clasp.

"Go ahead, Frank. You can open it. It's yours."

Frank sat next to him on the porch swing. "All right. That's so nice of you." He raised the lid. Inside the box velvet lining cushioned an antique gold and silver pocket-sized compass. The glass face was flawless. Floating in clear oil was a hand-painted face with tiny marks showing each of the 360 degrees. The N – S – E – W directions were lettered in bold black.

"I don't know what to say, Mr. Rigsby. This is awesome! I've never owned a compass. Are you sure that you want to give this away? There must be someone in your family that would want this."

"Nonsense, Frank," he replied, shaking his head. "I want it to be yours. You and your family have been so kind to me. I know *exactly* where I'm going when I say goodbye to this world, and I sure won't need this compass to get there whenever that day comes." He chuckled over his own words. "It's *yours* now, Frank. Use it and enjoy it!"

"Thank you very much. I *will* enjoy it, I'm sure." Frank paused and then changed the subject. "Mr. Rigsby, have you heard about the circus train that broke down late Tuesday night? There are probably over a hundred people stranded here until they can get it running again."

"Yes, Frank, I have. Earlier this morning, your sister Kate took me to the market, and I saw perhaps ten people there that I didn't recognize. From their appearance and how they dressed, I could tell that they were from the circus train."

Mr. Rigsby continued. "You and I know that they do back-breaking work, and most of them are respectable and honorable people. It made me sad to see some of our townspeople—many of whom I have known for years—snub them and look at them disrespectfully. I saw two women hold their noses as some of those folks passed those women inside the market."

He continued. "In the Bible in 1 Samuel 16, it says that 'The Lord sees not as man sees; because man looks on the outward appearance, but the Lord looks on the heart.' We should learn to do the same."

....

The Rialto Cinema was almost packed. Chase, Frank, and Griff had to climb to the second row from the back to find three seats together.

"I didn't expect half this many people," Griff remarked. "It's a good enough movie, but it's been out for a while, and I would have guessed more folks had already seen it."

"I don't recognize most of the people here," Chase added. "I think this audience is mostly from the train."

The lights began to dim, and the buzz of the crowd turned quiet. Frank leaned toward Griff and Chase and whispered. "The smell of that popcorn is just about to get to me, but I'm holding out for the pizza later, and lots of it, I hope!"

....

When the film ended, the house lights slowly came on, and the movie credits began to roll up the screen. The Bon Air boys waited in the upper row for their turn to exit the theater. Once outside, they stepped into the cooler, night air. The moviegoers assembled and moved like ants in clusters going in different directions. Many of them headed toward the fairgrounds, but the majority of them strolled away in the company of Faith Family Church members.

Earlier, when they met at the theater, Chase and Griff were each driven by their parents. Kate dropped off Frank. Now, at 8:00, the three friends were on their own, and they began the half-mile walk to Griff's house.

A block into their trip they reached the intersection of Stafford and Wellington Avenues. The streetlight there flickered and turned on as the boys waited for cars on both streets to come and go. When it was safe to continue, a flash of light reflected for a split second on something shiny on the sidewalk just ahead of them. Thinking it might be a coin or a piece of glass, Frank slowed and took a closer look. He stopped, leaned over, and picked up a flat oval of metal. There was a hole punched in an end, and through the hole a brass ring was looped!

"Guys, this must be the missing part from that key we found yesterday!" He turned it over and revealed the number C-11 stamped onto the tag.

"It sure looks like it," Griff agreed. "I think my dad will want this to go along with the key. *Now* he can find which locker it belongs to!"

They hurried their pace, more eager than ever to get to Griff's home and report their discovery. Within a half-block of their destination, a familiar car turned the corner ahead of them. It slowed and then stopped along the curb. It was Sheriff Lee Jenkins. He leaned across the front seat toward the passenger door and rolled down the patrol car window.

"Hey, fellows. Did you enjoy yourselves? Was the movie good?"

"It was, Dad. We're headed to the house for pizza. Are you going to your office this late?" Griff asked quizzically. "Is something up?"

"I'm afraid so, son. I just got a call from the Desk Sergeant. The manager of the circus is there now waiting for me. You remember him, I'm sure—that rather loud fellow from yesterday? He now says that the safe on the train was broken into. The payroll and the ticket receipts from the last two weeks are missing—$8,000 is gone. *It appears they were robbed!*"

....

A FLEETING FIGURE

Chapter 4

"That's awful, Dad," Griff agreed. He handed the metal key tag to Sheriff Jenkins. "We just found this on the ground, and we think it goes with the key we brought to you. They weren't on the same road, but here it is, anyway."

The Sheriff turned on the overhead light of his patrol car and examined the tag. He looked back at Griff. "I'm going to be short-handed around town for most of tomorrow. Deputy Reynolds is still on sick leave. If you'll take another good look at this tag, boys, maybe I can make all of you Junior Deputies just for the day. You can go to the bus station and train station to check out *their* tags and lockers," Lee Jenkins said with a twinkle in his eye. "Then, report back to me if *this* tag looks like the ones at either place, okay?"

"Sure thing, Sheriff!" Frank said excitedly.

"That's great! We can do it!" Chase agreed.

"If there's a locker C-11 and it doesn't have a key stuck in it, we're going to assume you have the key for it in your office. I'm guessing nobody has come forward to claim it, have they?" Griff inquired.

"No, son. Nobody at all." He glanced at his dashboard clock. "I'm sorry, but I need to be getting to my office. Let me know if you learn anything after you finish your detective work. Stay safe, boys. I'll be home later." Lee Jenkins smiled and pulled away from the curb.

"That's pretty cool that the Sheriff asked us to do official business for him!" a smiling Frank said.

"I don't think it's like *officially* official, but we can sure show him that he can trust us," Griff agreed. "Let's get to my house. The pizzas are probably there waiting for us. Nobody likes it when it's cold!"

....

The cloudless sky the next morning was an early sign that even for August, a sweltering day was ahead. The three friends met on their bicycles at 9 o'clock where Griff's driveway met Wellington Avenue.

"I brought my camera," Griff said, holding up the tan case with its shoulder strap. "You never know when you might need to get a photo of some evidence."

"That's good thinking, buddy," Chase agreed. "That's our motto: *Be prepared!*"

"The bus station is closest, so let's head there first," Griff suggested. "We'll be able to tell right away if the key we found matches any of those lockers. Let's get going!"

The bus station was two blocks from the town square, and a block over from Frank's dad's insurance agency office. They pedaled the eight blocks quickly and walked their bikes onto the covered loading platform. They parked them next to the newspaper rack and the vending machines.

The air smelled of diesel exhaust fumes from a Countryside Coach that idled nearby. Its lower compartments were open as a porter busily stowed suitcases and duffle bags in the luggage space. Small groups of people lingered near the bus's entry door while they said their farewells.

The inside of the station with its shiny benches and worn, oak floors smelled of old, varnished wood. The three friends crossed the lobby and stopped by the lockers at the end of the waiting area.

"I don't think this is where that key is from," Frank observed. "The numbers on these lockers don't include any letters with them. See this tag and the metal label. They start with "1" and go through "48". No A, B, C, or any letters are on these tags."

"Well, that makes it one down, and one to go!" Chase concluded. "Let's head for the train station."

"All right, but let me walk through here for a minute before we go," Griff suggested. "I want to shoot a few pictures to make a record of this assignment."

He stepped into a far corner of the room where he framed and focused a photo that included the whole area. Then from another position, he snapped several photos of various people on benches, the ticket counter, and the newspaper stand. A man's voice suddenly blared over the loudspeaker system announcing to those in the lobby that the Countryside Coach was ready to depart.

"Okay, I'm done here," Griff said. "Let's go check out the train station."

The rail yard and train station were three blocks farther away from town, and the boys covered that distance on their bicycles in only a few minutes.

"Hey, there's the circus train," Frank observed as they arrived. "You can't miss it! There must be twenty-five cars in the line!"

"Yeah, the engine looks like a toy way down the track," Chase noted, pointing into the distance on one of the rail yard's tracks.

"Let's see what we find in here," Griff said, leading the way through the double doors onto the marble floors of the Lewisville Train Station.

Inside the waiting area, a clock with hands at least three feet long was mounted high on a wall at one end. Every footstep, each door closing, or any bench creaking echoed loudly in the sunlit room.

The locker area was opposite of the big clock. Chase, Griff, and Frank walked in that direction, and their sneakers squeaked with every step on the polished floors.

"*These* numbers are like the key tag we found," Griff noted. He continued looking in the E's, the D's, and finally reached the C's.

"*It's missing! Locker C-11's key is missing!*" Frank tapped on the metal door. "That means something is inside here, and because *we* have the key, whoever put it in there can't get it out," he explained.

"Yeah, these tags look exactly like the one we found last

night!" Chase said excitedly. "Don't you wish we had x-ray vision like Superman? Then we could see whatever is behind that door."

Griff removed the cap from his camera lens. "Let me snap a photo of locker C-11, and then I'll take a few more pictures around the lobby. I want to be able to show my dad what we saw on our detective mission!"

"After you finish, how about we go check out the circus train? I'd like to see it up close," Frank suggested.

....

The rail yard was at one time in the past protected by a guard shack located next to a double gate. Now, no one was inside the shack, and the gate was not only wide open, but one-half of it had fallen off its hinges and was resting against the fence.

The boys cautiously entered. Twenty-five yards away stood the caboose. The crippled engine was several hundred feet farther down the track.

"What was that?" Frank uttered with an anxious whisper.

"I didn't notice anything," Chase replied.

"Something or someone just ran under the caboose," Frank stated. "It was either a small person or a big animal."

Frank squatted next to the caboose and looked between the sets of wheels. He shaded his eyes from the sun to better see into the shadows. He had an easy view to the other side of the track, but there was no one in sight—only gravel, spindly weeds, and open spaces.

"That is really strange," Frank said as he stood. "I *know* that I saw a figure of somebody just as they went from the daylight into the shadows. But there's nothing there—no one."

At that moment a muffled thud and mechanical click came from inside the caboose.

"I heard *that*!" Chase announced. "No question about it! It sounded like someone turned a latch or lock."

The three stood motionless watching and listening for any further movement or sound. After a half-minute Frank suggested, "Let's keep on going to the engine. We'll stop here again when we leave, and maybe we can figure out what made that noise."

The train cars smelled of axle grease, straw, and animals. As they continued walking, the boys saw no one around the track. The big locomotive looked imposing—like it could fire up, blow the whistle, and pull back onto the mainline. A ladder was leaning against the engine's right side. Several steam lines and an access panel were disconnected from the boiler. Power tools lay strewn on two levels of the scaffolding.

"I wonder if they're making any progress with it," Griff ventured aloud. "It would be a shame if the circus had to miss their next performance, especially without the money that was stolen."

The boys continued to the front of the steam engine and

crossed over the tracks. From there they began the walk back to the guard shack and gate. Once they had passed most of the train cars, they looked ahead and noticed a figure, mostly in shadows, crouching beneath the caboose. The face and features weren't visible, but whoever it was wore a multi-colored shirt and had a yellow cap or bandana. He stayed perfectly still, almost as if he was waiting for the boys to get closer—like he was challenging them to catch him.

In the last fifty feet, Griff sprinted toward the figure. When he did that, the person backed up beneath the train and *pulled himself up into the caboose through a trap door in its floor!*

"No you don't!" Griff shouted as he grabbed two legs dangling out of the opening. The person struggled, but Griff held on tightly. The other boys were only seconds behind their friend, and they helped to wrestle the stranger back down through the trap door and into the sunlight.

"You aren't supposed to be...." Griff stopped speaking and stared wide-eyed in amazement. *The stranger was a girl,* and she couldn't have been more than eight years old!

"You're not supposed to be around here, little girl! It isn't safe with all of this machinery and heavy things. You could get hurt! Where are you from? What's your name?" Frank insisted.

"Della."

"What's your last name?"

"Washington. I'm Della Washington."

"You need to go home and stop playing around the rail-road yard!" Griff demanded. "My dad is the Sheriff, and he wouldn't like it if he knew you were playing in here."

"But *I am* home," the small voice uttered. Tears began to fill her eyes.

"What do you mean? *Where* is your home?" Chase asked.

She pulled her small arm out of Griff's grasp and pointed one finger up at the train car. "I live right there."

....

THE WITNESS SPEAKS

Chapter 5

Griff was astonished. "I've never heard of *anyone* living on a train. Are your parents or someone else in the caboose now?"

"It's just me and Pa, and he's been gone since yesterday early."

The boys looked at each other puzzled and amazed, and all had the same thought: they *had* to help this little girl.

"Can we go inside and see where you live?" Frank asked.

Della Washington ducked back under the coach and stepped to the trap door. "Lemme climb up and open the door for you. You go to the back, and I'll let you in." She hoisted herself upward and disappeared into the hole. Immediately the boys heard the sound of bare feet hurrying to the rear of the car. Before the boys could climb the steps of the train car, she was waiting for them at the opened door.

Inside the caboose, the boys looked around the crude living quarters. At the front of the car were high and low berths for beds. A potbelly stove for heat in the winter and for cooking year-round was bolted to the floor. A supply of split logs for the stove was stacked next to it. Across the aisle was a clothes closet, a pantry, and a tiny room with a toilet. A metal ladder led to an observation window atop the caboose. That window gave a view to the outside in all directions.

Della sat down on the faded cushion of a bench seat. "Do you know when your dad is coming back?" Griff asked.

"All I know is when he left he said he wouldn't be gone long."

"What about food? Have you eaten anything today?" Chase questioned.

"Jus' some crackers. We don't have much food."

Griff turned to Chase and Frank. "Okay, guys, we can't just leave her here. It isn't safe, and she's gotta eat a real meal."

"I'll have Sally and my mom come," Chase offered. "They can take her to our house until we can find her dad."

Chase sat down beside the little girl. "Will you come to my house, Della? My mom and sister will take care of you until your dad comes back. It'll be safe, and you can get a bath. I know that there are some clothes in our attic that will fit you—ones that Sally used to wear."

Della sank even deeper on the cushion, and she turned away from them. Without saying a word, it was clear that she didn't want to leave the train.

Griff stepped close to the girl and picked up her small hand. "I'll tell you what, Della. Just come with us for a little while so you can eat a good meal. We can figure the other things out after that. We want you to be safe and back with your Pa real soon."

Della stood up. Her lower lip trembled, and she wrapped her arms around Griff's waist.

"Let's head back to the train station, guys. I'll call my mom from their payphone."

....

After Mrs. Spencer and Sally came for Della, the boys mounted their bikes and rode to the Sheriff's office.

"Is my dad here?" Griff asked the receptionist.

"Not at the moment. The dispatcher sent him out to the fairgrounds. There was a disturbance of some kind—a fight, I guess—and no one else was available to go. You can wait in his office if you'd like, Griffin."

"Thanks, but I think we'll just hang out on the front steps if that's okay."

"Suit yourself. He shouldn't be gone very long."

....

A patrol car arrived and parked in the space marked *Sheriff*. The boys stepped up to the driver's door as he opened it.

"Dad, there's a lot to tell you," Griff said eagerly. "We did some detective work like you asked. I think you're going to be interested in what we learned."

"Come inside, boys, and give me a minute to turn in some paperwork to the clerk. Then you can fill me in. Go ahead on into my office."

Lee Jenkins poured a cup of coffee while the boys settled into chairs across from the Sheriff's desk. He joined them, closed the door, and sat on the front edge of the desk. "Tell me what you learned."

Chase and Frank looked at Griff. "Well, the key tag came from the train station, not the bus station. We know that for sure."

Frank spoke next without missing a beat. "The circus train was in the rail yard on the sidetrack, and there was nothing going on. Nobody was working on the engine."

"But we saw a little girl by the caboose," Chase quickly added. "She lives *inside* of it, Sheriff. We could hardly believe it. She let us go in, and she told us that it's just her and her dad, except he left her alone yesterday and hasn't come back."

"Did you learn her name?" the Sheriff asked.

"It's Della, Della Washington," Griff replied.

Lee Jenkins stood, walked around behind his desk, and sat in his chair.

"My mom and sister came to the train station and took her to our house," Chase said. "She can't be more than eight years old. They'll feed her and, hopefully, give her a bath and some clean clothes."

"Boys, what I'm about to tell you can't leave this room. *Do not* talk about it with anyone else. Do you understand?" All of them nodded.

"You already know most of the story anyway. When you were here yesterday, you saw that man who was in my office yelling at me and telling me to arrest someone. His name is Marcus DeSilva, and he's the manager of the circus. The person he was insisting that I arrest was Ezekiel Washington. DeSilva is positive that Ezekiel Washington was able to get into the company safe, and that he is the person who stole the $8,000."

"Wow! So do you think that Della's dad has left town with that money—just left Della and isn't coming back?" Frank asked.

"I honestly don't know what to think. That would be terrible for him to actually do that. Washington works for the railroad, not the circus. Fletcher Railway owns the engine, the caboose, and a half-dozen train cars. The Bingham Circus leases space and pays for the rail services so they can be taken to the places they perform. The engineer, the fireman, the brakeman, and Mr. Washington work for Fletcher. The other three of those men have already gone to Lexington. They'll be there until the steam lines and boiler are repaired. Mr. Washington stayed here."

Lee Jenkins continued. "I didn't know anything about there being a daughter until hearing that from you three. In fact, the circus manager, DeSilva, didn't even know his first name. He just called him 'Washington.' I learned his full name when I spoke to some of the circus members while I was at the fairgrounds just now."

"Gosh, Dad, this is all pretty strange. The train breaks down and ends up in Lewisville. The circus people take their animals and belongings and set up their big tent. They're sleeping and eating at the fairgrounds. While the train is empty, someone opens the safe and steals all of their money. Ezekiel Washington is the person who stayed behind, and the circus manager says he's the thief. He's nowhere to be found, *and* his daughter gets left alone."

"Don't forget the locker at the train station," Frank added. "*Something* is in there, and we, I mean *you*, Sheriff, have the key."

"I need to speak with Della as soon as possible, Chase. Can you call your mom and ask if this is a good time to drop by?"

"Yes, sir. I'll call her now."

....

Sally Spencer sat on the sofa next to Della in the family's living room. Earlier Chase's mom offered her an adult-sized lunch, and the little girl ate almost everything in sight. She'd taken a hot bath and was now dressed in a floral print frock two sizes larger than she usually wore. Several safety pins helped to take up the excess fabric. At least Della and the dress were both clean.

"Della, I'm a friend," said Lee Jenkins in his softest voice, "and I just want to ask you a few questions. Do you know where your daddy went?"

"No, sir."

"Has he ever left you alone before?"

"Never, sir."

"Was anybody with him when he left? Did he go away alone?"

"I saw a man outside a lil' while before he left, but I don't know his name."

"Was he tall or short? Was he wearing anything unusual that you can remember?"

"He had a, what's that word—a mush-tash and he had a hat. My Pa is bigger than him. Pa calls him the circus man."

Sheriff Jenkins looked at Mrs. Spencer. "Is it okay if she stays here with you tonight? I don't know what else we can do with her."

"Of course. She can stay as long as she needs to. Sally is enjoying having her here."

"There are some very specific legal things that I will need to do if we determine that Della's dad has abandoned her or if he is actually missing. Since no one has reported him missing, I'm going to start the clock on that process now. We don't know if she is sure of when he left. I'll have one of my people inform Child Services this afternoon."

He stood and turned to Griff, Frank, and Chase. "Thank you, boys, for your work today. I'm going back to my office and prepare a search warrant and ask Judge King to sign it. I believe under the circumstances we have sufficient cause to believe that whatever is in the locker is evidence or certainly suspicious in this situation." He looked at his watch. "It's Friday, and the court offices will be closing soon. If I can't get the warrant approved this afternoon, nothing will happen until Monday. You are welcome to be there today or Monday when I open that locker—if you'd like to come."

"Yes, sir!" they all answered.

Sheriff Jenkins gently patted Della on the shoulder. "We'll get you back with your daddy, honey. It won't be long." He said goodbye to the others and walked to the front door. "I'll call the phone here, Chase, if I can get the warrant signed in the next hour."

....

Sally took Della up to her bedroom while Mrs. Spencer returned to the kitchen to begin preparing supper. The boys played two games of 9-ball pool in the Spencer's basement. They regularly checked the clock on the wall as the minutes of the 4 o'clock hour ticked away.

Once the hour passed, Griff noted, "I guess my dad couldn't get the search warrant in time. Whatever is in the locker will just have to stay there until Monday."

The basement door opened, and Sally came down the steps. "I don't know if this means anything or not, but Della's been napping. She's still lying down, but she's been talking in her sleep, and she keeps saying *'Pa don't go'*. Then she says over and over what sounds like *Smit's Grove*. You might want to listen for yourself."

The boys followed Sally up to her bedroom, and they quietly went in. The drapes were closed, and in the darkened room Della, her eyes shut, turned restlessly atop the pink bedspread.

"Pa, don't go! Smit's Grove. Stay here, Pa!"

Frank whispered to the others, "I agree with Sally. It's pretty clear to me, too." The four of them stepped out of the bedroom and into the hall, closing the door as they did. "Her dad must have gone to Smith's Grove. About the only thing over there is a truck stop. The quickest way, if you're walking, isn't an easy way. You'd take one of the marked trails near the east side of Perry State Park. It's probably a five-mile hike going that way."

"Yeah," Chase agreed. "By highway, it would be at least fifteen miles because you'd have to go around the outer boundary of the park."

"It's not a great trail anymore, either, since it's not very popular. It isn't maintained nearly as well as other parts of Perry Park," Griff added.

"How about we do this," Chase offered. "First, let's assume Mr. Washington *isn't* the thief and that he *is* coming back. We really ought to go back to the train and leave a note for him. He'd be mighty upset not to know where his daughter was when he returned."

"Agreed," said Griff. "We can do that right after supper. And, Chase, we'll put your phone number on the note."

"Good idea, and then," Chase continued, "if we don't hear anything from him tomorrow or by after church on Sunday, we can hike over to the Smith's Grove truck stop after lunch. It's mostly a flat route, and I think we can get there with no problem in a couple of hours."

"Yeah," Frank agreed. "Even if we spend an hour or two in the afternoon looking around at the truck stop asking people there about him, we can be home by sundown."

"That sounds like a plan," Griff said. "But tonight, let's meet at my house at 6:30. We can ride back to the train station and leave that note on the door of the caboose."

....

INTO THE FOREST

Chapter 6

Nearly a hundred Bingham Circus members and crew were staying as guests in the homes of Faith Family Church members. They slept in spare beds of their hosts. The church members washed their guests' clothes, cooked their meals, and even drove some around for different errands. Several Lewisville children learned from their guests how to juggle. Other children tested their balance on makeshift tightropes stretched between trees, a foot or two above backyard lawns.

The other thirty employees of the circus slept and ate at the fairgrounds. They stayed close to the animals to feed and protect them. Those circus workers bedded down under the big-top on cots provided by the National Guard from nearby Taylor County.

The Faith Family members agreed among themselves to provide a potluck supper meal at the fairgrounds on Saturday. They planned to feed all 130 Bingham Circus people along with the church families who were hosting them. Following the meal, they organized a brief church service under the big-top led by Reverend Metcalfe and the music director Gene Walters.

Chase, Griff, and Frank arrived at the church at 4:00 to help load the donated food into two vans. Scores of families prepared casseroles, bowls of potato salad, trays of fried chicken, and assorted home-cooked vegetables. By 5:15, five six-foot tables, placed end-to-end under the big-top, were filled with food. The circus cast members arrived with church families, and everyone convened near the food tables. Pastor Metcalfe stood on a folding chair to address the crowd of more than 300 people.

"Friends, it is good to see all of you again. This has been a difficult few days for many of you. But we at Faith Family hope that when you look back at this experience, you'll remember that you are loved—loved by a great Creator and by us. Would you bow your heads with me as I lead in prayer giving thanks for this food?"

"God, you are faithful to us. Everyone here understands that you never mismanage the lives of people who trust in you. You can do only good, so we look for the good that will come from this delay. Bless this food that we are about to enjoy. Amen."

While the circus members served themselves, Griff took the opportunity to walk through the tent and snap photographs of those in attendance. At 6:15, the mealtime ended, and everyone carried a folding chair and claimed their places in front of a portable stage. Soon enough, lively music began. Reverend Metcalfe stood and shared a short and meaningful devotional. By 7:30, the Saturday night church service was history, and most of the crowd had returned to their homes back in town.

....

"Mom and Dad, I'll be in the darkroom in the basement for a little while. I shot pictures yesterday and tonight, and I'd like to develop the film before I head for bed. Is that okay with you?"

"Yes, son. Keep up with the time so you don't stay there too long," Lee Jenkins replied.

As an amateur photographer, Griff learned from his dad the procedures for safely removing the exposed film from his camera, mixing the chemicals, and then turning negatives into photographic prints. This knowledge had come in handy in the past for him and his two best friends.

He prepared the solutions and filled the developing trays with the proper liquids. Griff then cut the developed roll of 36 pictures into four strips of nine photos each. The first strips of film were from the bus and train station. The others were photos he had just taken at the fairgrounds meal and the church service under the tent.

Griff switched the photo enlarger lamp on and slid a strip of film into place. An image that he captured on the negatives was now projected onto the enlarger table. A piece of white cardboard served as a background for the image. As Griff adjusted the height of the enlarger, he was able to zoom into a crowd of faces and focus on a single person.

He took the third negative strip and put the piece of film into the enlarger. It had been less than two hours since he snapped those photographs, and the faces of many of the circus people had become familiar to him.

Griff positioned the strip in the enlarger and slowly moved the negative holder to view the zoomed-in areas of the images. He stopped on negative #22. Something unusual caught his eye, and he carefully focused the lens. He leaned toward the white cardboard and squinted to be sure. As Griff made a slight adjustment of the focus, the photograph became remarkably clear. The image of a person he had not noticed before was on the enlarger bed in brilliant black and white. He looked slightly older, his shirt was different, his hair was a little darker, but *the person in the picture was nearly the twin of his friend Chase!*

Griff checked the remaining negatives on the film strip and didn't see that person in any other photographs. He put the second negative into the enlarger and spent several minutes examining other photos, but none of those photos included this young man, either. He then went back to negative #22, turned off the enlarger and under the red glow of the safelight he loaded an 8 X 10-inch piece of photographic paper and made a print of the negative.

Griff passed the paper through the trays of developer and baths, then removed it with a set of tongs.

He turned on the overhead light. It felt strange to see an older version of a person that he knew all of his childhood. It was very much like seeing Chase as a young adult.

....

"I put my largest canteen and some paper cups in my backpack in case you didn't think about it," Frank said. The three boys had been to church, and each ate their Sunday lunch in their homes before they met in Griff's driveway.

"You guys brought your walkie-talkie, I hope?" Chase queried.

Griff patted his backpack before he slung it behind him and mounted his bike. "Yep, and some chocolate bars for energy."

"Let's get going," Frank said. "Since we'll need to leave our bikes inside the forest along the trail, I packed a chain and padlock to wrap around a tree and keep someone from taking them while we're on our hike. I don't believe anybody would bother them, but it doesn't hurt to play it safe."

The peninsula of land in Perry State Park that was closest to Lewisville was within two miles of town. The walking trail that crossed through that part of the park was thick with trees. None of the boys had ever hiked that exact route, but before they met to leave, Frank studied a brochure with diagrams of the park. They all felt good about the trip. As Scouts, they'd had many day hikes and overnight camping expeditions in other parts of Perry State Park.

By 2:00, their bikes were hidden and secured several yards from the path. With that done, the boys joined the trail towards Smith's Grove. In the first half-mile, the painted marks were bold and clearly showed which direction to go. Stripes and arrows of white paint were brushed onto the tree trunks at eye level every 30 or 40 feet. If the boys looked down, it was hard to recognize any path. The Park Service had barely maintained this trail because the public wasn't using it much anymore. Without the white, painted stripes, the path would have been impossible to follow.

A woodpecker, somewhere in the distance, worked to hammer a hole in a tree for its nest. Once in a while, something unseen scurried through nearby leaves and underbrush. After thirty minutes, the landscape turned into gently rolling terrain, and the trees were farther apart.

Whispers In The Wind

"Let's stop for a minute," Griff suggested. "There's a rock in my shoe, and it's bugging me."

"I'm good with a quick rest," Chase replied. "There's a big tree trunk lying on the ground just ahead. We can catch our breath there."

Frank set his backpack down and wiped his brow with the sleeve of his t-shirt. "I've been thinking about Mr. Washington. The way Della cried and talked about missing him, it doesn't seem like he's a bad person."

"Yeah, but even good people can get desperate when they run out of money and have to feed their families," Griff stated.

"Since he and Della stayed with the train, they probably didn't realize our church was helping everyone with meals," Chase guessed.

....

The deep part of the forest was cooler by at least ten degrees than Lewisville had been. The tops of the trees swayed gently from an afternoon breeze moving into the area. As they neared Smith's Grove, the three of them could see much more sunlight between the trees in front of them. In the final hundred yards, they heard diesel trucks leaving and arriving at the truck stop. The whine of tires from passing traffic confirmed that they had finally reached the boundary of the state park.

The truck stop was active with dozens of 18-wheelers. The smell of diesel fuel and smoke filled the air. At the gas pumps for cars, they saw station wagons with rooftop luggage racks loaded with suitcases, ice chests, and folded tents. Family sedans arrived with children streaming across the parking lot in search of a restroom or the candy counter inside.

"This place is *really* busy," Griff said. "I can't imagine they'll remember one man who came here days ago!"

"Let's go in and try," Chase said.

They waited for the traffic to clear, and the Bon Air boys crossed the busy highway. They dodged vehicles that were coming and going on the asphalt lot as they approached the store. Frank reached for the door handle of the entrance. "This may be a wild goose chase, but at least we can check it off our list," he reasoned.

"The tough part is that we don't know what he looks like. All we have is his name," Chase lamented.

The cash register counter was six-deep with people waiting to pay for their fuel, comic books, or bottles of soda. The three friends stepped to the end of the line and slowly moved forward until it was their turn to face the talkative man and woman cashiers.

"I know that this is going to sound odd," Griff began, "but we're trying to find someone. He might have been here a few days ago. We're just not sure."

"What did he look like?" the lady asked.

"Well, actually, we don't know. His name is Ezekiel Washington, and we think he is sorta tall."

The two clerks looked at each other.

"He would have walked. He probably came here from the trail over there," Griff said, pointing to the state park across the highway.

"Was he meeting someone, or what?" the lady asked.

Before they could reply, the man cashier said, "I was outside changing the letters on the sign by the road—I guess it was on Thursday. Yep, it was Thursday around midday—and a tall fellow crossed the highway coming out of the woods. I remember it because a trucker just laid on his horn thinking the guy was going to step in front of him."

"*Yes!*" said Frank excitedly. "That could have been him."

"I saw that guy, too," the lady added. "He spent a long time talking on the payphone. I remember him because a truck driver got upset and asked me if we had another phone he could use. There's a second one by the highway, but it doesn't work. Your man came inside and bought a few groceries. I remember it because when he was leaving, his paper bag tore, and he came back and asked if we could double-bag it. He said he had a long walk to get back home."

"Did you see which direction he went?" Griff asked.

"It was busy at that time. It always is; and, no, I didn't notice," the man said.

"Thank you. This helps us," said Frank.

Outside the truckstop store, the boys compared thoughts.

"If he said '*Home—I have a long walk home*'—I wonder if he meant he was going back to the train," Chase asked.

"I'm confused," Griff began. "Today is Sunday. Della says he left her on Thursday. So he's been away for three days, and nobody else has seen him."

"It's safe to say he's not around here any longer. I think we should begin heading back." Frank looked at the sky and then his wristwatch. "Those clouds are really building up. If we can pick up our pace, we ought to get back before sundown, and we might beat any rain."

Chase, Griff, and Frank safely crossed the highway and entered the Perry Park trailhead leading back to Lewisville. Most of the trees there towered a hundred feet over their heads, and they quickly realized the sunlight reaching the forest floor was noticeably less than just a half-hour earlier. The paint marks on the trees were now red when headed southwest, instead of white as when the boys were hiking *toward* Smith's Grove. The coming darkness meant it was more crucial than ever to keep the paint marks in sight.

After thirty minutes on the trail, Griff exclaimed, "Listen to that wind up there!" All of the boys paused and looked to the treetops. "It's whipping them around like we're in for a serious storm!"

"Let's keep moving as fast as we can," Chase suggested. "It's getting to be almost like nighttime down here. I wouldn't have guessed that. Keep your eyes open for the paint marks. We'll need our flashlights before much longer. Did you guys bring yours?"

"I didn't," Griff replied.

"I did," Frank said.

Rumbles of distant thunder rolled through the treetops. As the boys tried to stay on the marked trail, Chase failed to see a paint stripe, and that mistake led them away from the trail. Flashes of lighting filtered down to the floor of the forest.

Chase stopped and shined his flashlight in front of him, swinging the beam around in search of the next red mark. "Guys, I think we're off the trail. I must have missed one of the paint marks. I don't know how far off we are, but we better back up and try to find the trail again."

No sooner had those words left his mouth than each boy felt an electrical charge in the air. The hair on their arms seemed to stand on end, and an explosion overhead sent a shock of lightning down a tree only a half dozen yards from where they stood. Bark, cinders, and sparks flew from the trunk—some landing just a few feet from the boys. The strength of nature's fireworks made their ears ring and nearly pushed the boys to the ground.

"We need to stop and get to the biggest clearing we can find!" Griff shouted over the howling wind. The rain was falling hard, and their damp clothes were now saturated. All of this made them chilled and miserable.

Frank slipped his backpack off and unzipped the largest compartment. "I have a piece of tent tarpaulin with me! It's been in here since our last Scout campout. We can use it as a shelter."

The three spread out the canvas and huddled and shivered together beneath it.

"Let me pray for us, guys," Frank said above the wind and driving rain. *"Dear God, we need your protection. We're trying to do something to help Della find her dad. Would you push this storm away and keep us safe? We need to find our way back home. Help us do that, too. Amen."*

The sound and feel of the raindrops began to lessen as the storm continued tracking away to the northeast. Thunder and the threat of lightning gradually eased as conditions improved. The wind continued to whistle overhead, and soon, the boys felt they could safely come out from their makeshift shelter. They stretched their legs while Frank shook raindrops off the wet tarp. He folded it and returned it to his backpack.

"Man, that was rough!" Griff said. "I've never been that close to lightning."

"That was the most scared I think I've ever been!" Frank agreed. "I'm glad I still had that tarp."

"Help me!"

"Huh? Did you hear that?" Frank asked.

"Please, help me!" It was the strained, breathy voice of a man.

"Yeah, but I can't tell where it's coming from!" Chase said anxiously. "The wind is blowing through here like crazy."

"Hurt. Need help!" said the frightened man with a hoarse

whisper.

Griff and Chase switched on their flashlights and pointed the beams urgently in all directions. Suddenly, just fifty feet away, Griff's light illuminated an arm and hand reaching upward from near the ground. All three rushed to that spot. *They were stunned to see a man lying on his back behind a massive, rotten log!*

....

MISSING EVIDENCE

Chapter 7

Chase was the first to reach the man. "Don't try to move, sir. We're going to help you."

Griff quickly sized up the situation. It seemed to them that the injured man stepped into the hole where a tree trunk once stood. Leaves and branches partially covered the hole. In the deep shade of the woods, it *looked* like the forest floor, but it was actually a deep pit. The man's forward motion broke his tibia, the part of his leg below his knee. After he fell, he was able to pull himself a few feet away from the hole, but there was no chance of him walking away. His leg was severely injured.

"How long have you been here?" Frank asked.

The man shivered and breathed rapidly as he replied. "I fell sometime on Thursday, so three days, I guess."

Within the first minute of finding him, Griff, Frank, and Chase all came to the same realization—the man was Ezekiel Washington.

With the storm ending and its clouds moving away, the late afternoon sun from low on the horizon made it only slightly easier to see. While the other two friends tried to keep him calm, Griff surveyed the ground nearby. He noticed a torn grocery bag and several spilled items beyond the reach of the man.

"We need to get you out of here and to a doctor," Chase said. "All of us know first aid, and we know how to help you."

The man's eyes filled with grateful tears. "I had just about decided that I was going to die here. I was never going to see my little girl again. *Thank you. Thank you for hearing me.*"

The boys knew that the only way to move Mr. Washington was to build a drag stretcher. They would use two sturdy branches and Frank's tarpaulin. Griff and Frank hurriedly searched nearby for limbs that were the right diameter and length —ones they could use as a frame for Frank's tarp. They collected vines as cords to keep the stretcher's frame of limbs from spreading too far apart.

Chase found some smaller branches that could use to stabilize the broken leg. He removed his outer shirt and tore his t-shirt into long strips. Chase then placed the small branches on either side of the leg and secured them tightly with cloth strips. Within an hour of finding Mr. Washington, they rolled him onto the stretcher. Griff and Chase each picked up one of the poles, elevating his head above his broken leg.

At this time, it was completely dark. The boys knew that they had wandered away from the marked trail *before* they sheltered under the tarpaulin. Then, finding Mr. Washington, they were still farther from the correct path. Frank held the flashlight and was ready to lead them out of the woods, but he was unsure which way to go. He stood frozen, thinking of what to do next.

"Wait a second!" Frank dropped his backpack, quickly

leaned over it, and shined his flashlight into one of the front compartments. "Look at this!" he said excitedly. "It's Mr. Rigsby's compass! He gave it to me the other day, and I stuck it in my backpack for safekeeping. This is amazing! I know *exactly* how to get us out of here, now!

The three boys took turns so that no one spent more than ten minutes pulling the stretcher. Ezekiel Washington was heavy, and the process was exhausting. Whichever boy was not dragging his stretcher pole took the lead and held the flashlight. All of them had learned how to navigate with a compass in their Scout survival training, so staying on the right path was the easiest part.

When they reached a point on the trail that seemed to be within a mile of Lewisville, Griff pulled his walkie-talkie from his backpack and began to call for help. "Breaker, breaker, we have an emergency—a medical emergency. Can anybody hear me? Over."

On his third attempt, a woman responded. "This is KPJ3504. What's your emergency?"

"My friends and I are in Perry State Park on the eastern trail heading south. We have an injured man that needs to get to a doctor. Can you please call the Jeffers Sheriff Office? The Sheriff is my dad. Ask him to meet us with an ambulance at the trailhead on Highway 311 near Lewisville. Over."

"10-4! I'm driving a truck, but I'm about to pull into a weigh station. There's a phone booth there. We'll get you some help! Over."

"Thank you. The three of us are fine, but the man with us

has a broken leg. Over and out."

....

Twenty minutes later, the boys saw the beams of several flashlights advancing toward them, sweeping back and forth from the edge of the forest trailhead. The boys heard Sheriff Jenkins' familiar voice call to them. *"Griff, we've brought you some help. An ambulance is waiting here. We're coming!"*

The exhausted friends stopped where they were, lowered the end of the stretcher, and waited for the rescue party to reach them. The roughness of the poles had cut into their hands. Their clothing, already drenched from the rain, was stuck to their skin.

Two neighbors from Bon Air Village and the two emergency medical people took charge of the stretcher and carried it to the ambulance. Frank, Chase, and Griff dropped to the ground, out of breath from the ordeal.

"Son, what happened? I knew that you all were going hiking this afternoon. Who is that man?" Lee Jenkins asked.

"We wanted to try to find Della's dad, so we hiked over to the truck stop in Smith's Grove."

Chase interrupted. "Della was talking in her sleep at our house, right after you spoke to her, and it seemed like she was saying for him not to go there. That was the only clue we had to help us figure out where Mr. Washington might be."

"We learned from the truckstop people that he *had* been

there," Frank continued, "but we missed him by three days. We were heading back home when that big storm came through..."

Griff picked up the explanation. "And in the middle of the storm with all the rain and the wind, we heard this man calling for help. That's Ezekiel Washington right over there," he said, pointing to the injured man being moved onto the ambulance's stretcher.

"My goodness! That is amazing, boys! Does he know about Della? Chase, did you tell him that she's with your family?"

"No, sir. We didn't say anything about her yet. We just knew that he needed help, and we got busy trying to get him out of there."

"Well, let's get your bicycles loaded in my trunk and get you three home. I am so proud of all of you! Your skills were sure put to great use tonight. You might have saved a man's life!"

....

Every joint and muscle in Frank's body ached. Lying on top of his bed blankets in gym shorts and a t-shirt, he listened to the faint sounds of his mother and Kate preparing breakfast. Kitchen cabinets opened and closed. Cookware clanked on the stove and in the sink.

He rolled onto his side so he could see his nightstand alarm clock. He uttered a groan as he felt the soreness that seemed to cover his entire body. *7:52.* He was sure that both Chase and Griff were hurting just as much from their time in the forest.

"Frank, are you ready for breakfast?" It was the muffled voice of his sister Kate coming through the closed bedroom door.

"I'll be there in a few minutes."

He slowly raised himself upright and swung his legs to the floor.

Once more, Kate spoke from the bottom of the stairs. "Griff and Chase are here!"

Astonished, he whispered to himself, *"Why in the world would they already be up and out..."* Before he could complete his thought, he heard the rumbling of four sneakers charging up the staircase. A few seconds later, his door burst open.

"Okay, Sleeping Beauty, we need you dressed and ready in, like, five minutes," Chase announced.

Griff continued. "My dad should have that search warrant for the locker by 9 o'clock. We want to be there when he goes to the train station to open it."

"How come you guys are already awake and so chipper?" Frank protested. "I can barely move!"

"It's all in the genes, buddy!" Chase retorted. "Naw, to be honest, I'm dying right now. Every inch of my body hurts, but I'm fighting through the pain." He grinned a toothy smile.

Griff responded to Chase's comment with a chuckle, and then he groaned. "Ouch! That hurts my ribs to laugh! But nevermind that, we need to get moving! Your mom invited us to stay for breakfast. Get some *real* clothes on and hurry down! The day is wasting, my man!"

....

On the driveway, the three boys mounted their bikes. "The courthouse opens in..." Griff checked his wristwatch, "...five minutes—at 8:30. My dad said if the judge doesn't have a full docket, he'll probably approve and sign the search warrant first thing. Let's go straight to his office and wait for him there."

....

The boys turned into the Sheriff's Office parking lot and parked their bikes behind the building. They walked back to the front steps and sat down.

"I wonder how Mr. Washington is this morning," Frank remarked. "He looked pretty bad when they put him inside the ambulance under those bright lights."

"I can't even imagine how helpless he must have felt for those days," Chase added. "When we were pulling his stretcher, I tried to put myself in Della's place. To be a little girl with no mother and then to have your dad missing like that—that's pretty awful. It was a miracle that we were there in that exact spot and that he heard us *and* we heard *him*."

"Yeah," Frank continued. "We were definitely off the marked trail, but it was so cool how God used our mistake to find Mr. Washington! And then to have that compass with us at the exact time we needed it! Wow! *That* was another miracle!"

At 8:55 the Sheriff's patrol car drove into the parking lot and stopped in front of the building. The boys stood and walked toward it. The windows were closed, and the engine idled while inside Lee Jenkins spoke with someone on his two-way radio. He looked through the glass at the boys and held up a single finger as if to say, *"I'll be another minute."* After three minutes went by, the boys sat down again on the front steps. Two more minutes passed, and he turned off the motor and opened the car door.

The Sheriff's expression was intense as he motioned to them while he climbed the steps of the building. "Come inside, guys. I need you to wait in my office while I handle something."

The chimes in the clock tower a block away above City Hall rang through the morning air as the boys passed through the doorway. It was 9 AM. They weaved past a half-dozen desks in the outer office area and stepped into the Sheriff's private office. Frank closed the door behind them, and the three friends sat facing the desk. Nobody spoke.

After a few minutes, the door opened. The Sheriff walked to his chair and dropped onto it with a sigh. "Guys, I thought that we would hear from the judge and be able to check on the locker at the train station this morning. Unfortunately, that's not going to happen. The conversation I was having on the radio in my car was with Deputy Reed. It seems that sometime overnight, someone went into the train station and used a crowbar and a hammer on the locker. They broke it open, and whatever was inside is now gone."

The boys looked at each other in disbelief.

He continued. "The one *sure thing* that we can now know is *whatever* was in that locker—and I suppose all of us figured it was the money—it wasn't stolen by Ezekiel Washington. He's laid up in the hospital. He *can't* be that thief."

....

NOT WELCOME HERE!

Chapter 8

Sheriff Jenkins scanned the boys' faces. They were visibly discouraged.

"That blows up our theories," Frank said. "I don't guess there were any witnesses that saw who did it, were there?"

"No. The night cleaning crew swept the floor by the lockers a little after 11:00. They finished their work at the train station before midnight. My deputy spoke with the person in charge of the workers, and she said that nothing was different last night from any other night. It happened between when they left at 12 o'clock and when the ticket window opened at 5:30. The outside doors of the building are never locked."

"Gee, we're kind of back to square one, I guess," Chase commented. "The only good part of everything that's happened is that Della got her dad back. She was *really* excited when I got home last night. I woke her up to tell her. My mom is taking her to the hospital this morning at 10:00 to visit him."

"*Oh, no!*" Frank exclaimed. "I'm supposed to help Mr. Rigsby at 10 o'clock. I totally forgot. I gotta get home and change into work clothes."

Chase turned to Frank. "I guess there's no reason to stay in town now. Griff and I can head back to Bon Air with you."

"Actually," Griff said, "I'd like to ride out to the fairgrounds and poke around a little. I have some questions I need to settle in my mind. I'll catch up with you guys later."

"I'm sorry that you made the trip here for nothing," the Sheriff said to them. He turned to his son. "Don't get tangled up with any wild animals out there," Lee Jenkins teased as he again mussed up Griff's curly hair.

....

Two blocks into his bike ride, Griff heard a familiar car muffler rumbling behind him. He steered his bicycle to the curb, came to a stop, and looked over his shoulder. It was Donnie, Chase's college-aged cousin.

Donnie eased his royal blue, two-door Chevy coupe alongside Griff and leaned toward the open passenger window. "What's happening, Griff? Where are you headed?"

"Hey, Donnie," Chase replied. "It's been a pretty strange couple of days, and this morning things got even *weirder*. I'm headed out to the fairgrounds to do a little detective work."

"I was out of town over the weekend, and I missed the Saturday night meal and the church service. You want to put your bike in my trunk and let me drive you there? I've kinda wanted to see the setup they have."

"Sure. I don't have a real plan in mind. I just thought I'd look around a little bit."

In another moment, they were underway, and Donnie began the conversation. "I heard that Chase is a hometown hero with that runaway train the other night. That's pretty neat."

"Yeah, and that was just the beginning of the strange things. Last night Frank, Chase, and I helped out a guy who had broken his leg when he stepped into a hole in Perry State Park. His daughter was sorta abandoned on the train when that man left town. Now she's staying at Chase's house while her dad recovers in the hospital. Man, *a lot* has happened! Some of the things I can't even talk about."

The upper half of the red and white big-top tent covered much of the horizon as Donnie and Griff reached the final hill approaching the County Fairgrounds. The sounds of elephants and lions seemed strange when a person usually saw cows and heard tractors along the route. The smells from the animal pens and wheeled cages greeted them through the open car windows as they entered the property. The odors nearly took their breath away.

Donnie parked at the edge of the tent, and both of them exited his car. "Hey, you two!" The voice came from behind them in the direction of a circus wagon where tickets were sold. The speaker was a burly, bearded worker wearing overalls and a straw hat. His mud-coated shoes and weathered face told Griff and Donnie that this man had probably worked outdoors for much of his life. "Nobody's supposed to be out here. We ain't open for business."

"I know," Griff replied respectfully. "My dad is the Sheriff, and he said it would be okay. We're not going to bother anything. We're just looking around."

"Well, I don't want you two going near the big cats. They

are funny about strangers."

"We won't. Don't worry," Griff replied. They continued walking toward the shade of the big tent.

Of the thirty people who were staying with the animals and tending to them, a dozen were reclining on the borrowed military cots. Beyond the tent, another half-dozen men stood by a rolling lion cage. One of its wooden wheels lay on the ground, and a worker was on his back under the axle, tapping on it with a hammer. The onlookers were offering advice to him.

"This is pretty amazing," Donnie said, "but this isn't everyone, is it? There *have* to be more people than this to put on a circus!"

"Oh, yeah—there are close to a hundred other people who came as the crew and the cast. They're mainly staying in the homes of people from our church. I've heard some cool stories about some of the kids learning how to juggle and stuff. We've fed them all right here—two times since Wednesday."

Griff and Donnie left the shade of the big-top and walked to a row of animal cages. Two men were nearby, rehearsing tricks with three, frisky show dogs. Past them, one man was spreading out bales of hay, the feed for the elephants.

Donnie suddenly blurted out, *"That looks like Chase. What's he doing here?"*

Twenty-five yards in front of them a young man held a water hose over a large trough. He was the person Griff had seen in the photographs he took on Saturday night!

"It's not Chase, but I definitely see the resemblance," Griff whispered. "Just older, but he looks a lot like him." Griff spoke in the direction of the fellow. "*Eric?*" The young man turned to face Griff.

"You two need to leave—now!" Griff and Donnie whirled around to find the rude man who had been in the Sheriff's office the morning after the train arrived.

"We were just..." Griff began to explain before he was interrupted in mid-sentence.

"This isn't any place for kids. *I want you out of here!*" He pointed toward Donnie's car. The man's hand trembled, and his face was red with anger.

"All right. We'll go," Griff said.

Before walking toward Donnie's car, Griff looked over his shoulder in the direction of the water trough. The young man was nowhere in sight.

....

The two drove away from the circus tent, and once they reached the main road, Donnie stopped his car and turned to Griff. "All right, something about that man seemed really odd. He wasn't just mad that we were *there*. It felt to me like he didn't want us to *see* something—like we were getting close to somebody or something that we aren't supposed to know about."

"I had the same feeling. His name is Mr. DeSilva, and I've

seen him once before. He was in my dad's office the morning after the train arrived, and he was pretty upset then, too. He had that look in his eyes just now like he recognized me, but something about him is *definitely* not right. I just have no idea what it could be."

Donnie turned onto the highway that led back to Lewisville. "So tell me about the guy that looks like Chase. What's *that* story?"

"Honestly, I don't know, but he is one of the reasons that I wanted to go there and look around today. He showed up in a photograph that I took during the meal before the Saturday night church service. I *guess* he's been in town from the beginning. His dad came looking for him and couldn't find him on Wednesday—that first time we took food to the circus folks."

As they entered the Lewisville city limits, Griff asked Donnie, "Would you drop me off at Chase's house? Frank is helping Mr. Rigsby this morning, and I'd like to tell Chase what just happened to us."

"I sure can. Let me know if you come to any conclusions or if I can help you guys at all."

....

Griff lifted his bicycle out of Donnie's truck and walked it the length of the Spencer's driveway. He lowered its kickstand near the garage, then tapped on the frame of the screened back door.

"It's open, Griff. Come in."

"Hi, Mrs. Spencer. Is Chase home?"

"He's in his room. You're welcome to go on up. Would you tell him that I'll have lunch on the table for Sally, Della, and him in about 15 minutes? You are welcome to stay and eat with us if you'd like."

"I'll tell him, and yes, I'd like that. Thank you."

When he passed through the living room and reached the stairs, he saw Sally and Della watching television with their backs to him. He quietly climbed the steps and pushed his friend's bedroom door open.

Chase was propped up on the lower bunk bed against two pillows. His feet were planted on the bed, and his knees were bent upward. A notepad was propped against his legs. Chase glanced at Griff and then pointed with his pencil toward the desk nearby.

"Grab that chair and roll it over here. I've been listing the things that we've learned so far about the train, the different people, and the missing money."

"Yeah, well I can add one more thing to your list because of what just happened to me."

"Really? Like what?"

....

Sheriff Lee Jenkins tapped gently on the door of Room 112 at Jeffers County Hospital. He waited for a response, then looked toward the nursing station. Supervising Nurse Shirley Bass nodded her approval. He slowly pushed the door open. Ezekiel Washington was lying on his side facing the window. Hearing the creak of the door, he rolled onto his back, opened his eyes, and managed a faint smile.

"Hello, Mr. Washington. How are you feeling so far this morning?"

"Good morning, Sheriff. I can't say that I slept more than about thirty minutes between somebody taking my temperature or checking my blood pressure. But everyone's been nice to me, and I'm sure not complaining."

"You had some rough days," Lee Jenkins said. "We're just glad that you are safe and can start to mend now."

"I can't thank those boys enough for being there. One of them is your son, right?"

"He is, and all of them are pretty amazing guys. They're Scouts, and I'd say they must have been listening when they were studying for their first aid badges. I'm proud of each of them." Lee Jenkins moved to the foot of the bed and continued speaking. "Would you mind telling me about being in Perry State Park? I want to get a better idea in my mind about you and Della, beginning with the time the train came into town."

When the Sheriff mentioned Della's name, Ezekiel's eyes widened, and his face brightened. "I got to see her this morning. She's staying with the Spencers. She is such a precious girl. She's my sunshine."

"They're good people, and she seems to be enjoying herself with Sally and the family. But when you left her alone, where were you going?"

"Sheriff, I'm not in any trouble, am I? I make sure that Della is doing her reading and writing. Two of the ladies with the circus are working with her every day with her lessons. They tell me she does good with her lessons. She's a smart girl."

"Mr. Washington, what I want to know from you is where you were going when you fell down in the forest. Why did you leave Della by herself?"

"When I left her, it was only supposed to be for a few hours, and she wasn't by herself then. A lady, one of the ones that teaches her, she came to our train car right when I was leaving. Sheriff, I didn't know until I saw Della this morning that the circus man came a few minutes after I started walking. The man told the lady that she couldn't stay with my girl or she would lose her job. That circus man doesn't like me. He's been talking bad about me to the railroad folks."

"Is Mr. DeSilva the circus man you're talking about, Mr. Washington?"

Ezekiel Washington nodded.

"I need to tell you, Mr. Washington, that he came to me the first morning after the train arrived here, and he wanted me to arrest you. He's accused you of breaking into the safe on the train and stealing $8,000."

Ezekiel Washington sat forward in his hospital bed. A frightened expression crossed his face, and he began to shake his head. "No, sir. *No, sir!* I didn't do anything of the sort. I *never* would do that. He came to me at the train that morning and said that I'd been messing with the safe. Sheriff, it's *Mr. DeSilva* that I've seen bring expensive things back to his train car when we stop in different towns. I told him that morning if any money was missing, it must've been him that took it. He knows that I know what he does. *That's* why he wants me fired from the railroad. *That's* why I went to the truck stop. I had to get away from here and call my brother. He always knows what to do. I didn't know who I could trust in this town."

....

ENCOUNTER AT DUSK

Chapter 9

Frank finished mowing the final rows of Mr. Rigsby's yard and returned the lawnmower to the storage shed. He closed the door and snapped the padlock in place.

The elderly gentleman stepped onto the back porch of the three-story home. He held a tray containing two glasses and a small plate. "Come on up here, Frank. Cool yourself off with some lemonade and a slice of pound cake."

"Thank you. I think August is hotter than July was," Frank commented as he wiped his brow on his t-shirt sleeve and sat down on a wicker chair. "It'll be nice when the temperatures begin to cool down, but we probably still have a few months before we can look for that."

"I believe you're right about that," Mr. Rigsby agreed, "although I don't look forward to cold weather like I used to. These old bones can't seem to warm up much anymore. Frank, after you were here the other day, I have been thinking about the people from the circus—how you said that some of our townspeople looked down on them and complained about them being here. The Bible has some strong words for us about our attitudes and how we give preference to some people and not others. In the Old Testament in Deuteronomy, it says, *Show no favor to anyone; judge everyone by the same standard, no matter who they are.*"

"Gosh, Mr. Rigsby, I knew that it seemed wrong when I

saw those people act hurtfully to the circus members. I didn't realize that the Bible talked about that, too."

"It surely does, Frank, and there are many more scriptures about being kind to everyone. When people look or speak differently than we do, or maybe their skin is another color, or they grew up in a different culture or country, then we often have the attitude that we are right and so they must be wrong. But God loves each person individually. He loves the train full of circus workers just as much as He loves you or me."

"Thank you for reminding me of that," Frank said. "My buddies Chase and Griff and I are trying to help the Sheriff with something. I really can't talk about what's going on right now, but would you pray for us—that we can find out the truth about a certain situation? I know that it will help."

"I surely will. I'll pray for you now, and I'll continue praying for all of you until you discover whatever you need to know.

....

It was just past noon as Frank mounted his bicycle and left Mr. Rigsby's. The route home took him past Chase's house, but when he saw Griff's bicycle standing near the garage, he quickly turned in. Frank parked his bike next to the one of his friend. When he reached the top step of the back porch, before he could knock, Carol Spencer spoke through the screen door. "Come in, Frank. I saw you through the kitchen window. The boys are upstairs. I'm serving lunch in a few minutes. Would you like to stay and join us?"

"Yes, ma'am. Thank you! I'll go on up. Thanks, Mrs. Spencer."

Frank could hear the muffled but excited voices of his friends as he neared the top of the stairs. He tapped his knuckles on the door, turned the knob, and stepped into Chase's bedroom.

"Hey, Frank. We were just going through a list of things about the case of the missing money," Chase explained. "Griff and Donnie went to the fairgrounds this morning. Mr. DeSilva wasn't thrilled to see them."

"Actually, he invited us to leave—like *quickly*! But here's something that seems odd to me, and I haven't told you yet, Frank." Griff continued to speak as Frank sat down on a wooden chest in front of the window. "There is a guy in one photograph I snapped on Saturday night. He looks a lot like Chase except he's older. Same hair, same height, and pretty much the same face—just older. He must work for the circus because he was watering the animals this morning when we were there."

"Yeah, when Griff and Donnie started to talk with him," added Chase, "that's when Mr. DeSilva came along and told them to leave."

"That's interesting, but I don't get what that has to do with the robbery or with Mr. Washington, or anything," Frank questioned.

"I want to go back there tonight and try to talk to him," Griff said. "He looked right at me when I said the name *Eric*. If his last name is Schneider, I think I should tell him that I met and spoke with his dad. He might not realize that anyone is looking for him. Would you two go with me—maybe after supper?"

At that moment, Connie Spencer spoke up the steps and through the door. "Lunch is ready!"

The three friends stood. "I'm game. You want to leave from my place at 7:00?" Griff suggested.

"Sounds good," Frank said.

"Me, too," Chase concurred.

....

At 7:05 PM one red and two blue bicycles rolled out of the Jenkins' driveway and turned west, headed for the County Fairgrounds.

"My dad told me that it looks like the train repairs will be finished sometime tomorrow," Chase said. "Some men from the railroad yard were in his store today talking about it."

"It's going to feel strange when all of those people are gone. A lot of families from church have made some nice friendships with the people who stayed in their homes—friends that they might not ever see again," Frank stated.

"Well, my dad was talking at supper tonight about the missing money," Griff added. "He said that the case is probably never going to get solved. He's convinced that Mr. Washington didn't steal anything, but Mr. DeSilva won't give up on having my dad charge him with the robbery. He keeps insisting."

"What about Della? Will she and her dad leave town when the train leaves?" Frank asked.

"I don't know. Mr. Washington is supposed to use crutches for at least a few weeks. I don't see how he can do his job with that cast on his leg," Chase speculated.

They pedaled the next two miles in silence. The sounds of the animals and the sight of the lighted big-top reached them as they turned off the main highway and onto the dusty and bumpy field of the fairgrounds.

"Let's park our bikes at the line of trees, and hopefully we won't run into Mr. DeSilva," Griff suggested. "The sun won't set for another twenty or thirty minutes, and I think we should lay low until it's a little bit darker."

"Good idea, buddy," Chase agreed.

"Where exactly was Eric when you saw him?" Frank asked.

Griff pointed beyond the big tent to a line of wheeled cages. "You can see a stack of hay bales over there. He was giving water to the horses by the last pen. *Hey! I think that's him now—right over there!*" he said excitedly.

As the boys watched from the edge of the field in the shade of the tree line, a slim figure walked the width of the red and white tent. The string of lightbulbs that crisscrossed under the big-top shined on a young man that closely resembled Chase. In a few seconds, he exited the lighted area and reached the shadows of early evening. He was quickly gone from sight.

"Let's hurry to that spot but stay next to these trees. We

can work our way over to where we saw him," Frank whispered. "Hopefully he's alone, because we may not get another chance to talk with him."

The three friends ducked in and out of bushes and trees that formed the perimeter of the field. Soon they reached the last animal pen. A bridle tie-down rope was stretched tightly between two steel posts that were driven into the ground. There were four horses spaced along the rope, secured by their bridles and reins. Water and hay for each horse were on the ground in front of them. The young man, his back to the boys, stood fifty feet from them, patting the shoulder of a chestnut-colored horse.

As the three boys inched their way closer, a horse heard their footsteps, and one whinnied nervously.

"*Eric!*" Griff called softly.

"Who's that!" Eric snapped back. "Who's there?" He looked in the direction of the boys and strained to see them in the light of dusk.

"It's Griff Jenkins. I was here this morning and saw you before Mr. DeSilva made my friend and me leave."

Eric Schneider ducked under the bridle rope and met the approaching boys. "Yeah, I remember seeing you, but how do you know my name? Why did you come back?"

The boys by now were face-to-face with the young man. Eric looked at the three of them and paid particular attention to Chase. He no doubt saw the resemblance himself, but then turned to Griff and waited for an explanation.

It was Chase who spoke. "Eric, I met your dad." He waited for the young man to respond.

Eric stared past the three boys and into the trees. He turned his head to one side, lowered his chin, and took a step back. He seemed to be in deep thought for another few seconds, and then he looked at Chase again and asked, "When?"

"It was that first afternoon after the train came—when our church brought a meal to the fairgrounds for everyone. We were unloading the food, and he offered to help me lift one of the containers."

"Actually Chase saw him earlier that day," Frank offered. "He was in town when we were there, and he noticed your dad in two different places."

Eric lowered his eyes and turned away from the boys. "What did he say about me?"

Chase responded, "He said that he'd been looking for you—that you had left home and he didn't know where you had gone. He wanted to find you. Before he left, he asked me to be on the lookout for you."

Eric focused on Chase as he continued speaking. "I think the reason he spoke to me and not to my friends was because he said I reminded him of you. It seemed to make him sad."

"So he didn't seem mad or anything?"

"Oh, no. Not at all. He had been trying to catch up with the train and the circus because he heard somewhere that you might have gotten a job with them," Chase explained. "He stayed around for a while, and when he didn't see you with all of the workers, he left the fairgrounds when we left."

Eric stepped away for several seconds and looked at the horses, the big-top, and then he turned back to the boys. "I was afraid I had blown it for good with him and my family! I made some dumb choices back home, and then instead of facing up to them, I just walked out. I knew where they kept some cash. I took some clothes and some of my parents' money. After I got my first paycheck with the circus, I mailed back to them what I took, but I figured they were probably finished with me."

"I can tell you one thing, Eric," Chase began, "there was nothing in his voice or in his face like that. He just hoped to find you again."

"Eric, we didn't see you when our church came here and brought that first meal. Where were you?" Griff asked. "I saw you on Saturday night, but not on Wednesday."

"Mr. DeSilva had me go back into town and look for something of his. He said he lost something important that morning when we took the animals from the train to the fairgrounds. He sent me back to look for it. I walked all the way into town and back but didn't find what he lost. I didn't get back to the fairgrounds until after you guys were gone and everybody had eaten lunch."

"You weren't looking for a key by any chance, were you?" Griff asked.

A puzzled look crossed Eric's face. "How did you know?"

"V" MARKS THE SPOT

Chapter 10

Suddenly from across the big-top, the four of them heard a door close. A man dressed in dark clothing walked down the steps of the ticket trailer, and then he disappeared behind it.

"That's Mr. DeSilva. He doesn't need to see you here," Eric whispered.

Not knowing where he had gone or if he was headed their way, the four pressed tightly against the closest animal cage. They froze and waited for the man to come back into view. In a half-minute, he reappeared, this time with a shovel. He paused and looked in all directions. Under the big-top at the far end were several men involved in two different card games. Their laughter and loud conversation indicated that none of them had noticed DeSilva or the shovel he was holding.

DeSilva eased away from the lights of the big-top and continued to the edge of the clearing. He walked toward the trees that bordered the fairgrounds, looking over his shoulder often. Frank, Griff, Chase, and Eric saw him continue to the end of the field and then slip between trees into the darkness of the forest. Once there, he switched on a flashlight. Its beam swayed back and forth with each of his steps until the man and his light completely vanished.

"Come on!" Griff exclaimed as he stepped away from the animal trailer. "This looks *very* suspicious! We can't afford to lose sight of him!"

"Where are you going?" Eric asked anxiously. *"He can't know that you're here. It would be..."*

"Don't worry about that—and just trust us! Let's go, guys! Come with us, Eric!" Frank urged.

The four of them hurried in silence to the place along the north line of trees where Mr. DeSilva had entered the woods. They paused there to regroup. From that location, they could barely see the light from his flashlight beam. In silence, they advanced toward the light, but stayed well behind him. For the next five minutes, they tracked him still deeper into the trees. When he finally stopped, DeSilva shined his light up and down a large, double-trunk oak tree that had grown in the shape of a "V." He placed his flashlight on the ground, leaned the shovel against the tree, removed his outer shirt, and began to dig.

The boys slowly closed the gap between them and him, taking a step each time he drove the shovel into the ground. When they were within fifty feet, they held that position and stayed low with a perfect view of the scene.

In another moment, DeSilva stopped digging, leaned the shovel against the oak tree, and knelt over the hole. When he stood up, he grabbed the light and pointed it at a maroon backpack he'd lifted from the ground. He brushed the dirt from it, put on his outer shirt, and slipped the backpack on. With the flashlight in one hand and the shovel in the other, he turned and began to walk *directly toward their position!*

The boys felt a wave of panic. They realized that for DeSilva to return on the path he'd taken into the woods, he would need to walk toward them. Then, without warning, he veered off in a different direction.

"What's he up to now?" Frank whispered. "That's not the way back!"

"I don't know," Griff whispered in reply. "I think he's disoriented. Let's stay with him. Thank goodness for the crickets all around, or he'd hear us for sure!"

The three boys and Eric let DeSilva get a hundred feet in front of them, and for several minutes they kept that separation from him.

Suddenly, they heard a frightened yell from the man. The flashlight beam swung wildly as DeSilva backed up and fell to the ground. He stood to his feet and began to walk forward, this time at a different angle. *"Aaaahhhhh! Noooo!!!"* he yelled.

The boys and Eric couldn't see what was causing his outbursts. The four of them stood perfectly still and waited. DeSilva started to walk forward again.

"Nooooo! Get off me! Get off me!" He spun around and stepped back again. The beam of his light almost hit the four when they finally realized the reason for the man's fears. Hanging between the trees, ten feet wide and just as tall were giant spider webs. They were everywhere, and the spiders waiting in them were as big as a man's hand! Mr. DeSilva had walked directly into one, and its silvery web was stuck to his clothes and hair!

He dropped his flashlight, shook off his backpack, and

slapped his shoulders, chest, and legs to brush off any and every possible spider—real or imagined. He muttered words that the four couldn't fully hear or understand. Then he picked up the dropped things and turned 90 degrees from where he had been standing.

The new course brought him back to the original path he'd taken into the woods. The boys remained crouched behind the underbrush until DeSilva was almost out of view. Then they carefully followed him until he arrived at the field with the big-top. They waited in the cover of trees until they could see his silhouette reach the ticket office. At that point, he climbed the steps, entered the trailer, and closed the door behind him.

"I think all of us have figured out what just happened," Chase said.

"My dad needs to know about this. He'll probably want to come out here tonight," Griff added.

"What are you two talking about?" Eric asked.

"We can't say for sure, but there's a whole lot of Bingham Circus money missing," Frank explained. "Griff's dad is the Sheriff, and DeSilva tried to blame the robbery on a man that we believe had nothing to do with it. We think that's what's in the backpack—the ticket money and the payroll."

"Hey, when we first got here I noticed a payphone over by the restrooms," Chase offered. "We can call your dad from there."

....

The three friends and Eric crept silently to the building that housed the restrooms. Griff pulled a dime from his jeans pocket, dropped it into the payphone, and dialed his home number.

"Dad, we're at the Fairgrounds. We think you need to come. We just followed Mr. DeSilva into the woods and watched him dig up a backpack. He's now in his office again." There was a pause as Sheriff Jenkins asked a question and then gave some instructions.

Griff replied. "It looks like he's by himself. Okay, we'll stay out of sight and wait for you."

....

"Do any of you have another dime?" Eric asked the boys.

"I do," said Chase, and he handed him the coin.

"Thanks. I need to make a phone call. It's one that I should have made weeks ago. Excuse me for a few minutes, okay? It's long-distance and collect, so I can give your dime back to you."

The three boys stepped away from the payphone and walked towards the fairgrounds entrance—out of hearing range.

"That's very cool," Frank said with a satisfied smile.

"What's cool?" Chase asked, also smiling.

"You know," said Frank.

The headlights from a familiar car swept across the fair-grounds. A second set of lights followed, and the two patrol cars silently came to a stop. As Sheriff Jenkins emerged from his vehicle with his revolver in hand, Griff got his father's attention and pointed at the ticket office. The Sheriff quietly climbed the steps of the office and knocked on the trailer door. The two deputies positioned themselves nearby. In a matter of minutes, Lee Jenkins emerged with a handcuffed DeSilva and a dusty backpack containing the missing $8,000.

"He'll ride in the back seat with my deputies. Between their patrol car and mine, we can fit your three bikes in the trunks. Are you guys ready to head back to town?"

"Give me just a minute, please," Chase said with a smile. "I need a word with my *twin* over there at the payphone."

Chase waited for Eric to finish his call and then walked toward him. After he hung up the telephone receiver, Eric lifted his t-shirt to dry his eyes. "My dad told me that he and my mom love me and they forgive me," a red-eyed Eric said. "I'm not going on with the circus tomorrow. I'm going to catch a bus in the morning back to where I used to live. They want me to come home."

"That is awesome, Eric! All of us make mistakes, but when we own up to the things we've done and really commit to change, God is always ready to forgive us and give us a new start! I'm so glad that your parents didn't give up on you—and that I got to see all of this happen."

Lee Jenkins spoke towards Eric and Chase. "We need to

"V" Marks The Spot   92

go, Chase—as soon as you can!"

Chase nodded toward the Sheriff. Eric opened his arms wide and gave the young, new friend a bear hug. "I can't thank you enough, Chase, for coming here tonight to find me."

"That's okay. It's what we're all supposed to do—encourage each other. You're getting another chance. And I bet you'll help someone, too, someday.

....

HOMEWARD BOUND

Chapter 11

Chase kept his eyes closed and breathed deeply. He tried to pretend that he didn't feel anyone tapping on his shoulder. After a pause of a few seconds, a small hand tugged on his arm. *"Chase! Chase, wake up!"* He raised his head and turned toward the voice.

"Della, can you come back later? I'm really tired, okay?"

"But Chase, I'm leaving now, and I wanted to say goodbye."

Chase rolled onto his side, forced one eye open, and squinted into the daylight. Della had on the same yellow dress she was wearing on the day the boys first met her, but this time it was starched and pressed. Her hair was brushed and held a bright pink ribbon. Her little face glowed with excitement. "They said my daddy is better, and we can leave with everyone on the train today."

The thunder of multiple footfalls on the stairs distracted Chase, and in a few seconds, his two buddies walked through his bedroom door.

"Are you going to sleep all day, or are you gonna come with us to be there when the train leaves?" Frank teased. "They're supposed to pull out of the station at 10:00, and it's a little after 9:00."

"Half the town will probably be there," Griff added. "They started moving the animals at sun-up, and I'll bet they're just about finished by now."

Chase threw off the blanket and sat on the edge of his bed. "All right, give me a few minutes, and I'll be right down."

"Your dad is bringing Mr. Washington by here to get Della," Frank said, "and they'll ride together to the station. Your mom said she'd drive the three of us. We'll see you downstairs." Frank walked to the door, stopped, and then pointed to the desk. "You and that shortwave radio of yours started something crazy last week. Who would have guessed all the things that have happened since then. Good job, buddy!"

....

The streets of downtown Lewisville were unusually busy, and the atmosphere among the people was more like a carnival than a workday. Pedestrians filled the sidewalks. Cars occupied every parking place around the town square as well as up and down the side streets.

"We're going to need to park behind the hardware store and walk the rest of the way," Connie Spencer said. "I don't think I've ever seen this many cars and people downtown."

As they walked the four blocks to the train yard, they joined scores of Faith Family Church members carrying suitcases and knapsacks of clean clothes belonging to the many circus cast and crew members.

"There's Kate and Mr. Rigsby!" Griff exclaimed. "Hey! Can you believe all of these people?" he asked Kate as the three boys and Mrs. Spencer caught up with Frank's sister and their family friend.

"It's amazing that our town reached out to so many who were once total strangers," Mr. Rigsby remarked, "and now it is time to say goodbye. It will be hard to see them go."

"I'll never forget this past week!" Griff exclaimed. "It's been awesome to have met so many interesting people, and to be able to help them when they needed it."

As the six of them approached the train station, they could see the coal smoke billowing, filling the sky above the rumbling, black engine. Two hands suddenly came down on the shoulders of Chase and Griff as a familiar friend stepped between them from behind. "I knew I'd find you guys here." It was Chase's cousin, Donnie. "I heard that they caught the guy who stole the payroll."

"Yeah. It's a shame that people can be that greedy. He tried to ruin Mr. Washington's reputation, but it was Mr. DeSilva that will pay the price for that."

As the crowd pressed toward the rear of the train, Reverend Bill Metcalfe climbed the steps of the caboose. He was holding a megaphone. In a moment, the friendly chatter subsided, and everyone gave him their attention.

"Good morning, friends. I've been asked to say a few words to the people of the Bingham Circus and you citizens of Lewisville. Since last week we've had the privilege of opening our town and our homes to folks who arrived as strangers. They are different from us in some ways but just like us in many others. Everyone, at one time or another, will come to the place where he or she has a need and has no way to go forward without a helping hand. That's what happened here. Instead of seeing these good people as outsiders, we saw them as our guests. We fed them, we offered them our spare beds, we washed their clothes, and we loved them. They gave us their friendships and their appreciation. Now as they go, we bless them. Would you bow your heads with me as I offer a prayer?"

"Dear God, just as you extended an invitation and an open door to everyone who comes to you, we thank you for the opportunity to do the same to these fine people. Now, as they leave us, we ask you to bless them and keep them safe. Don't let us forget these days or how it feels to do good unto others. Amen!"

Across the crowd of hundreds, a dividing line began to form. The circus cast and crew drifted toward the train and climbed aboard. The townspeople stepped away from the tracks and onto the train platform or the gravel of the rail yard. In another few minutes and without warning, the steam whistle of the iron engine let out a long blast followed by an earth-shaking thud as the line of cars began to move.

"Chase! Hey, Chase!" A voice from somewhere behind them rose above the thunder of the train engine and the commotion of the crowd. *"Over here!"*

The three friends turned toward the voice to see Eric Schneider dodging people as he weaved a path through the crowd, his hand held high in the air. He stepped up to Frank, Chase, and Griff.

"My bus leaves in 15 minutes, but I came here hoping I'd see you guys before I left. The way you three supported me and cared about me—I'll never be able to fully thank you for it."

"That's how people are supposed to respond, Eric," Griff said. "We were just doing what anyone should do."

"I know, but I had to tell you thanks before I left."

"Well," Frank said with a grin, "now that you know where we live *and* that Lewisville is a good place to be if your train or your car is going to break down, come back sometime and hang out with us again!"

"Yeah," Chase agreed, "but if you hadn't come here just now, I was about to head for the bus station to find *you*, because the best I can remember, *you* still owe me my dime."

Mr. Rigsby laughed. Kate appeared puzzled, and the other two Bon Air boys shook their heads and turned away in disbelief.

"Oh, *I* didn't forget," Eric said as he reached deep into his jeans pocket. "Here's a whole roll of dimes for you, Chase. I wrote my phone number on the cardboard tube. Call and check in with me in a couple of weeks and I'll tell you how it is when you get to have a fresh start to your life!"

One by one, the boys and Kate hugged Eric as the train slowly rumbled out of the yard, its whistle declaring a very hopeful note.

········

Whispers In The Wind

A FEW MORE THOUGHTS...

Frank learned from Bible verses told to him by Mr. Rigsby that God loves each person. It doesn't matter if you are tall or short, thin or heavy—or from Africa, Asia, or America. God created everyone and everything. He loves you and them just the same. You and I should do that, too.

Someone once said that we don't have to *like* everyone, but we ought to *love* everyone. You probably won't do this automatically, but it will take place when you decide to have this attitude. Not all of the people in your school or where you live will become your close friends, but because they are important in God's eyes, they should be accepted by you as valuable. Love them (be kind and considerate of them) even if you don't expect to be their best friends. You never know if someday you might need someone who doesn't sit by you at lunchtime to help you when you've fallen down and can't help yourself!

We met Mr. Schneider when he came to the County Fairgrounds trying to find his son. Then, we learned from Eric what had happened that made him think he needed to leave his home and family. We realized from this situation the unconditional love his dad was demonstrating.

The two words that I want you to learn from this part of the story are *sin* and *grace*. When Eric got angry and stole some of his parents' money (even though he later repaid it), those things were wrong—they were *sins*. He left home, but soon the money in his pocket was gone. He had said hurtful things to his family, but they still missed him and never stopped loving him.

When Chase met Eric's dad, it was because Mr. Schneider had learned that his boy might have taken a job with the Bingham Circus. He was faithful to search and keep searching until he could find Eric and tell him that he was welcome to come home again. This is *grace*, and it is part of the character of God. He seeks us even though we aren't looking for Him or paying attention to Him.

Eric's story reminds me of how we, as humans, have *sinned*. Our heavenly Father, God, doesn't want us to live apart from Him, His blessings, and His provisions. Because of His *grace*, He seeks to bring us back "home" into a relationship with Him.

I don't want you ever to think that you have wandered too far from the heavenly Father. He will always welcome you back.

Greg Golden

Be sure to enjoy other
Bon Air Boys Adventures

The Secret Of Hickory Hill
Lights On Wildcat Mountain
(and more!)
available from Amazon.com
Also available
as Kindle E-Books

Stay connected with
The Bon Air Boys
and the author by visiting
BonAirBoys.com
There you will find the latest information
about upcoming books and products.

Made in United States
Orlando, FL
22 December 2021

12371027R00069